MEMORANDUM

To: Audrey Finnegan, my most alluring—
and *temporary*—new secretary

From: Wheeler Rush, your slightly confused boss!

Re: I can't seem to forget you....

Ms. Finnegan,

Attached please find a proposal designed to renew your tenure here indefinitely. Your secretarial skills are somewhat…rusty. Nonetheless, Ms. Finnegan, I find myself unable to get you off my mind.

You see, Ms. Finnegan, the attraction here is not just your sea-green eyes, your ivory complexion— or your body that just won't quit. It's the way you've taken hold of my heart—and that despite your claim that bad luck seems to follow you wherever you go, I've had nothing but good luck since you crashed—um, *walked,* into my life.

Therefore, I respectfully request that you accept my proposal—and its accompanying engagement ring. You see, Ms. Finnegan, I happen to love you.

Yours sincerely,

Wheeler Rush

Dear Reader,

Silhouette Desire matches August's steamy heat with six new powerful, passionate and provocative romances.

Popular Elizabeth Bevarly offers *That Boss of Mine* as August's MAN OF THE MONTH. In this irresistible romantic comedy, a CEO falls for his less-than-perfect secretary.

And Silhouette Desire proudly presents a compelling new series, TEXAS CATTLEMAN'S CLUB. The members of this exclusive club are some of the Lone Star State's sexiest, most powerful men, who go on a mission to rescue a princess and find true love! Bestselling author Dixie Browning launches the series with *Texas Millionaire*, in which a fresh-faced country beauty is wooed by an older man.

Cait London's miniseries THE BLAYLOCKS continues with *Rio: Man of Destiny*, in which the hero's love leads the heroine to the truth of her family secrets. The BACHELOR BATTALION miniseries by Maureen Child marches on with *Mom in Waiting*. An amnesiac woman must rediscover her husband in *Lost and Found Bride* by Modean Moon. And Barbara McCauley's SECRETS! miniseries offers another scandalous tale with *Secret Baby Santos*.

August also marks the debut of Silhouette's original continuity THE FORTUNES OF TEXAS with Maggie Shayne's *Million Dollar Marriage*, available now at your local retail outlet.

So indulge yourself this month with some poolside reading—the first of THE FORTUNES OF TEXAS, and all six Silhouette Desire titles!

Enjoy!

Joan Marlow Golan
Senior Editor

Please address questions and book requests to:
Silhouette Reader Service
U.S.: 3010 Walden Ave., P.O. Box 1325, Buffalo, NY 14269
Canadian: P.O. Box 609, Fort Erie, Ont. L2A 5X3

ELIZABETH
BEVARLY
THAT BOSS
OF MINE

SILHOUETTE *Desire*
Published by Silhouette Books
America's Publisher of Contemporary Romance

SILHOUETTE BOOKS

ISBN 0-373-76231-3

THAT BOSS OF MINE

Copyright © 1999 by Elizabeth Bevarly

All rights reserved. Except for use in any review, the reproduction or utilization of this work in whole or in part in any form by any electronic, mechanical or other means, now known or hereafter invented, including xerography, photocopying and recording, or in any information storage or retrieval system, is forbidden without the written permission of the editorial office, Silhouette Books, 300 East 42nd Street, New York, NY 10017 U.S.A.

All characters in this book have no existence outside the imagination of the author and have no relation whatsoever to anyone bearing the same name or names. They are not even distantly inspired by any individual known or unknown to the author, and all incidents are pure invention.

This edition published by arrangement with Harlequin Books S.A.

® and TM are trademarks of Harlequin Books S.A., used under license. Trademarks indicated with ® are registered in the United States Patent and Trademark Office, the Canadian Trade Marks Office and in other countries.

Visit us at www.romance.net

Printed in U.S.A.

Books by Elizabeth Bevarly

ELIZABETH BEVARLY,

who marks her twenty-fifth book with *That Boss of Mine,* is an honors graduate of the University of Louisville and achieved her dream of writing full-time before she even turned thirty! At heart, she is also an avid voyager who once helped navigate a friend's thirty-five-foot sailboat across the Bermuda Triangle. Her dream is to one day have her own sailboat, a beautifully renovated older-model forty-two-footer, and to enjoy the freedom and tranquillity seafaring can bring. Elizabeth likes to think she has a lot in common with the characters she creates—people who know love and life go hand in hand. And she's getting some firsthand experience with motherhood, as well—she and her husband have a four-year-old son, Eli.

For David and Eli,
my good-luck charms

One

Wheeler Rush braced his elbows on the top of his desk, buried his face in his hands and bit back the barrage of obscenities he really, really wanted to shout. Loudly. On the other side of his desk, in the posh office on a *very* desirable block of Main Street in downtown Louisville—an office for which he'd signed a lease less than nine months ago—stood two men leaving scattered, colossal footprints in their wake. Two men, he noted as he looked up again, whose brawn genes had exceeded their potential.

The larger of the men, the one who had identified himself as Bruno—that was all, just…Bruno—shifted his massive weight from one beefy foot to the other and scratched the back of his head. At least, Wheeler thought it was the back of the man's head. Having no neck that way, and with all that scruffy hair springing out from the open collar of his shirt, Wheeler supposed it could have been his back the man was scratching.

"Look, buddy," Bruno said. "We don' wanna hafta do

this, but we got no choice. When you can't pay the money you owe, this is what happens. It's that simple.''

"I won't submit to this kind of terrorism," Wheeler insisted, feeling much less confident than he sounded. "Leave now, or I'll call the police.''

"It ain't terrorism," Bruno assured him. "This is bidness, plain and simple. You can't call the cops. You don' have a leg to stand on." He cracked his knuckles menacingly, suggesting that Wheeler really wouldn't have a leg to stand on, once the other man broke it. "You hear what I'm sayin'?" Bruno continued. "Now stand up and move away from the desk. Hey, you brought this on yourself, pal. Be a man about it, for God's sake.''

Wheeler narrowed his eyes, hating to hear his manhood impugned in such a way. The last thing he wanted to do was submit to these two goons, but what else could he do? Bruno and company had come for a specific purpose, and they weren't going to leave until their work was complete. Sick to his stomach, he realized he had no choice but to do exactly as they had instructed. He simply should have shown better judgment in the beginning, when he'd gone into business for himself. Instead, he had played too fast and too loose with money that wasn't his, and now he was going to have to face the consequences.

"Listen, buddy," Bruno growled again when Wheeler still hadn't risen, "I'm sorry for your unfortunate professional downturn, but I got a job to do like any other guy, okay? And me and Harry here got a long day ahead of us. Now stand up and move away from the desk. Don't make us get ugly.''

Wheeler clamped his lips over the retort that threatened to leap from his mouth, then, reluctantly, he stood up and did as Bruno had requested. "Fine," he muttered a bit more gruffly than he'd intended. He ran a restive hand through his dark brown hair, tugged anxiously on his necktie and jerked his dark suit jacket from the back of his chair. "Let's just get this over with. Whatever you do, *please*...don't get ugly.'' Or rather, he amended to himself, ugli*er*.

Bruno and his missing-link companion stepped forward, stretching their arms out fiercely, and instinctively Wheeler flinched and took a step in retreat. When he did, one man grabbed one end of his desk and the second hefted the other end. Then, effortlessly, the two of them lifted the massive, and very expensive, teakwood, art deco piece of furniture and carried it out the door, presumably into the waiting truck that held the rest of Wheeler's expensive, teakwood, art deco ex-furniture.

He watched the repo men go, and sighed as if they'd just carried out a childhood friend, feetfirst. Now the contents of his desk and filing cabinets would have to remain against the wall in a long row of cardboard boxes cast off from the wine shop below his newly rented apartment.

The apartment, he recalled, that was barely a tenth the size of the elegant, old, brick Victorian he'd called home as recently as a few months ago. The old, brick Victorian on Tony St. James Court, he further reminded himself ruthlessly, that he'd been forced to sell for less than it was worth in an effort to save his fast-sinking business. Now Wheeler lived in a cramped studio on the top floor of a battered old Federal in the borderline Original Highlands neighborhood.

Damn.

He'd had such high hopes when he'd gone into business for himself. Now, barely nine months after having his name etched in the glass on the outer office door, Rush Commercial Designs, Inc. was already going belly-up.

''Mr. Wheeler?''

He turned his attention to the open door of his office. The unmistakably feminine voice that called out from the reception area beyond was unfamiliar.

''It's Mr. *Rush*,'' he replied automatically, wearily, his irritation at having his last name used as his first rising nowhere near as quickly as it usually did when that happened. Which was often. "Wheeler Rush," he added under his breath. When no one came forward at his summons, he cranked up the volume on his voice a few decibels. "I'm in here!"

Just as he shouted the announcement, a woman's head appeared in the open doorway, about halfway down, as if she were bent at the waist. A shock of blue-black curls was caught at the very top of her head, a few errant corkscrews dangling about her face and neck, the rest of it bobbing wildly from the source of its confinement at her crown. Huge, round sunglasses covered her eyes, and her lips, the color of autumn apples, formed a perfect O.

"Can I help you?" he asked on a halfhearted sigh.

The woman smiled and straightened, then stepped into the doorway. He stifled a gasp when he noted her attire. A very brief, very snug, very red miniskirt hugged her hips, and an even briefer, even snugger, even redder sweater clung to her torso. The combination was big enough to cover what a woman needed to cover in polite society, but not big enough to hide a bare strip of creamy flesh that peeked out between the top and bottom parts of her ensemble. A huge red straw bag, sheer red stockings and red high heels completed the outfit.

Wheeler blinked a few times, as if doing so might tone down the color a bit. But when he opened his eyes to consider the woman again, she was still…red. Really, really red.

"Actually," she said, her smile growing broader, "I think it's me who's going to help you."

Try as he might, he couldn't for the life of him pull his gaze away from her legs. But then, seeing as how just about every inch of leg was visible—and quite a number of very shapely inches there were, too—that wasn't altogether surprising.

"I beg your pardon?" he finally managed to ask.

As he watched, those legs began to approach him, the miniskirt at their tops hitching higher and higher with every step forward the woman took. When he darted his gaze back down toward her ankles, he noticed, too late, that she was heading straight for a bump in the lavender-and-yellow dhurrie rug that must have sprung up when Bruno and company left with the last of his repossessed furniture. Before Wheeler could warn the woman to watch her step, her toe connected with the bump, and her body went sailing forward.

She had been extending her hand to him in greeting when it happened, and as she fell, she must have instinctively bent her fingers as if groping for something to grab onto. The action resulted in what basically amounted to her punching Wheeler right in the stomach before she crashed to her knees before him.

He doubled over—more from surprise than from pain— at the impact of her fist driving into his belly right about the same time she began to push herself up from her position on the floor. As a result, their two heads collided with enough force to send the woman back down to her knees and Wheeler snapping backward.

With a quick shake of his head to clear it of its stars, he reached down—gingerly this time—to lend her a hand. But she chose that moment to glance up at him, an action that would have resulted in him poking her in the eye had it not been for her ridiculous sunglasses. Instead he only knocked them from her face, and they went clattering to the floor between them.

Wow.

That was the only thought that came into Wheeler's head when she looked up at him again. Whoever this red woman was, she had the greenest eyes he'd ever seen. Pale green, like the shallowest part of the ocean, but deep enough to drown a man if he wasn't careful. Framed by long, sooty lashes and topped with elegant ebony brows, they completely overpowered the rest of her face.

For a long moment he could do nothing but stare at those incredible eyes. Then finally he managed to recapture his balance and the presence of mind to take in the rest of her features, as well.

Pretty.

That was the second thought that went through Wheeler's mind when he considered her. Really, really pretty. Her ivory complexion was smooth and flawless, a hint of pink riding high on her finely chiseled cheekbones. Her lips—as red and inviting as her outfit—were full and ripe and luscious. And something inside him knotted tight at the sight of her, kneeling there before him in a manner that was in no way appropriate for two strangers. With no small effort, he finally kicked himself into gear and extended a hand cautiously toward her.

As if she were feeling just as wary as he was, she scooped up her sunglasses, then slowly lifted her hand to tuck her fingers into his. Gently, Wheeler tugged her back to a standing position, then pretended he wasn't noticing as she shoved her skirt and sweater back into place. But he couldn't quite ignore the scant inch of bare skin that peeked out at him from between the waistband of her skirt and the hem of her sweater. And whatever had knotted tightly inside him grew even more taut, nearly cutting off his breath, wrenching a strangled sound from deep inside him.

"I'm sorry," she said softly as she gave her sweater one final yank.

Something inside him rejoiced, however, when the sweater bobbed back up again, once more exposing that sleek line of flesh. "No problem," he replied automatically.

The woman lifted a hand—which he noted absently was decorated with long, red nails and two big Band-Aids—to the curls still dancing wildly about on her head. Then she smoothed her fingers ineffectually over the mass, which bounced right back the moment she completed the gesture, and smiled. "I'm Audrey. Audrey Finnegan? I'm the office temp you requested."

Wheeler was so caught up in contemplating her flat abdomen that he scarcely heard what she said. "Office temp?" he repeated idly.

"From One-Day-at-a-Timers," she clarified. "You called them Friday needing someone to start on Monday? Today, I mean?"

It was a question not a statement, and vaguely, way back at the back of his brain, he realized she was waiting for an answer. But, still far too preoccupied by the sight of Miss Audrey Finnegan, all he could manage in that respect was, "I called them Friday?"

Somehow he nudged his gaze from her body to her face, and he realized he'd been doing her a grave disservice to focus on her midsection. As appealing as her torso was— and mind you, it was extremely appealing—her face was infinitely more interesting. Even when she was squinting at him in utter confusion the way she was now.

"Didn't you call them Friday?" she asked. "Isn't this Monday? And isn't this Rush Commercial Designs, Inc.? Or did I come to the wrong place again? I'm pretty sure this is Monday? Isn't it?"

Did he? Had she? Was it? Oh, yeah, Wheeler finally recalled, shoving his libido to the side. This was definitely Monday, and she'd certainly come to Rush Commercial Designs, Inc. At least, it was still Rush Designs, Inc., for the time being. And he had called for a temp Friday. Right after he'd given his regular secretary, Rosalie, her walking papers and two weeks' severance. That on the heels of letting go his two associates last month.

As much as he'd hated to lose his staff, Wheeler simply wasn't able to pay their full salary and benefits anymore. Hell, he couldn't even pay his own salary and benefits anymore. It was going to strain his newly reworked—and very minuscule—office budget just to have a temp working. But he didn't have a hope in hell of salvaging his failing business by himself. He was going to need someone to run the day-to-day basics of the office while he focused on his clients and accounts, even if that someone was just a temp.

Clients and accounts, he muttered to himself. Yeah, right. Like he was going to have any of those left by month's end. They were disappearing faster than leisure suits.

He still couldn't figure out where he'd gone wrong. When he'd been employed as a commercial designer by a much larger conglomerate, Wheeler had had more work to keep him busy than anyone else at the firm. His designs had been very much in demand, and he'd risen fast and far on the corporate ladder. So fast and so far, in fact, that one day, a year ago, he'd decided to strike out on his own. Hey, he'd built himself an excellent reputation, he'd reasoned then. Why give all the credit to a company that wasn't his own?

So he'd struck out solo, bringing a number of his old firm's clients with him. And at first, everything had gone fabulously well. He'd exploded with creativity, had introduced design after design that was cutting edge and savvy. He'd garnered new clients in addition to the old, and had expanded to handle all the new business, hiring two associates to help field their accounts. Rush Commercial Designs, Inc. had left the starting gate at an amazing pace and had been trotting effortlessly right toward the finish line. Until a few months ago, the future had been rosy and warm.

Then...

Well, Wheeler still wasn't sure what exactly had gone wrong. He'd come home from a long business trip with the flu and had been out of the office for two weeks. In his absence, however, his associates had fared just fine. At least he'd thought they were faring just fine. But upon his return, things hadn't seemed to run quite as smoothly as they had before. Granted, it had been January, something of a slow month for the business, but still…

His work shouldn't have come to such a grinding halt the way it had. He'd tried to tell himself it was just one of those slumps that occurred in all types of businesses every now and then, and that they would ultimately pull through it none the worse for wear.

But they didn't pull through it. The slump became a downturn, and the downturn became a stagnation. One by one Wheeler's clients had become disenchanted with his ideas. And with every parting account, he had started to feel less and less creative. Ultimately his brain—once a playground for generating original, clever ideas—started to dry up. What few concepts emerged from the muddled pool of his creativity were tired, standard, clichéd. And then, even his most faithful clients began to slink quietly away.

It made no sense. In addition to being talented, smart, ambitious and driven, Wheeler Rush had always been just about the luckiest man alive. He'd been born into a close-knit, loving family, one that had never hurt for financial well-being, one whose members were all intelligent, successful, attractive. Not a day of his life had passed that he hadn't reflected on what a genuinely fortunate person he was. He'd never wanted for anything. He'd always achieved whatever he set his mind to achieving, effortlessly at that. Never once had it crossed his mind that he would be anything but a massive success in life.

At least, it hadn't crossed his mind until his business had started to go belly-up. Then he hadn't been able to avoid thinking about his potential for failure. Miserable, humiliating, vicious, rotten, crummy failure.

But that was all about to end, Wheeler told himself now. He was sure of it. Well, pretty sure, anyway. Sort of. In a way. Yes, he'd had to make some serious sacrifices to keep himself from going under. He'd been too overconfident in the beginning, and he wasn't going to make that mistake twice. He'd pared down what had been an excessive office budget from the start. Hey, you had to spend money to make money, right? Wrong. His newly adopted motto was you had to save money to make money. And that was what Wheeler would do.

Hence, Miss Finnegan. At minimum wage and no benefits, she was a real bargain. The minute he got his business up and running again—and Wheeler vowed then and there that he *would* get his business up and running again—he could hire back his old staff at their old salaries, provided they were available. If not, he'd hire some new blood. Hey, maybe if Miss Finnegan worked out, he thought magnanimously, he could keep her and Rosalie both.

For now, however, Rush Commercial Designs, Inc. was going to have to work with a two-man team. Or rather, a two-person team. If there was one thing Audrey Finnegan most definitely was not, it was masculine.

"So, where should I start?" she asked when he still had offered no clear answer to her question. Evidently she had decided for herself that she was needed here.

Wheeler looked around. Yeah, he could understand how she would feel that way. No furniture, no clients in the waiting room, no phones ringing off the hook. He definitely needed something. Or somebody.

What the hell, he thought further. For now, Audrey Finnegan would do.

As Audrey stood waiting for an answer to her question— and an answer to any of her questions would do, she thought as she waited some more—she took in her new boss from the tips of his Italian loafers to the tousled dark brown hair atop his head.

What a cutie, she thought. Truly tall, dark and handsome, with broad shoulders, trim hips and chocolate-brown eyes to just curl up and die for. Maybe after twenty-eight years her luck was about to change.

Nah. Who was she kidding? Audrey Finnegan was the most totally jinxed person on the planet, and a new job wasn't likely to change that. She should know. She started a new job just about every month, and they all ended the same way—badly. But she'd been unlucky all her life—at cards and at love and at everything else—so she wasn't going to stand here and try to kid herself that things would ever change in that department.

Just this week alone she'd lost her job, her boyfriend, her apartment, her car and her cat. Roxanne, the silver tabby she'd adopted a few months ago, had taken up with a no-good tomcat and hadn't come back. Audrey's car had been totaled after the emergency brake had finally given out when she'd parked on a too-steep hill—the old VW bug had rolled downdowndown, crashed into a power pylon and gotten fried into blackened Beetle au gratin.

Then, as if that weren't enough, her basement apartment had been flooded during a surly spring downpour, ruining all her furniture and forcing her to shack up temporarily with her best buddy, Marlene, with whom she'd never really gotten along. And although Audrey thought she'd been doing great at her job as a grocery store cashier, coming up short fifteen thousand dollars and change that night just didn't look good on a person's permanent record.

And as for her boyfriend, well, she would just as soon forget about him. There was nothing like having a guy tell you you were cold as a dead fish to make you think twice about getting involved again. Of course, Brad hadn't exactly been a pep-rally bonfire himself, Audrey reminded herself, which was only one of the many reasons she'd avoided becoming too intimately involved with him. Still, a woman liked to think that a man would have *some* regrets about dumping her. But Brad, evidently, would always think of her as sushi.

So with all her bad luck of late—and of her whole life—Audrey didn't really expect that a change of jobs would do anything about the dark cloud of misfortune that had followed her everywhere she'd ever gone from the day she'd been born—breech and thirteen days late. It was a family curse, common knowledge. All the Finnegans were unlucky, all the way back to her great-grandmother Fiona Finnegan, who fell off the boat that arrived in New York Harbor at the turn of the century.

Literally. She fell off the boat, right into the water. It had been the beginning of a looong line of Finnegan bad luck. Klutzy, ditzy, jinxed, hexed—those were all words that Audrey had heard used to describe her family over the years. And, carrying on the family tradition, she, too, was little more than a bad-luck charm. Wherever she wenteth, mishap followedeth. To put it in the vernacular, she, like the rest of her family, was not exactly a child of fortune. Nothing ever went right for the Finnegans.

Still, she reconsidered as she eyed her new employer, maybe she was due for a spurt of good luck for a change. If nothing else, Mr. Wheeler would be infinitely more appealing to look at than Manny the bag boy had been.

"Um," he said, by way of response to her earlier question about where to begin. "I suppose I could show you around the office."

Audrey arced her gaze around the room, taking in one elevated design table with halogen lamp, one high stool of unmistakable saloon origin and numerous boxes holding numerous files. It wasn't much different from what she'd encountered in the outer office—one generic desk with off-off-*off*-brand computer, and more boxes full of files. "Okay," she said, wondering what more there might be to Rush Commercial Designs, Inc.

"This," Mr. Wheeler said, throwing his arms open wide, "is my office. That—" he waved a hand toward the design table "—is my work area and is *not* to be touched under any circumstances. Those—" he gestured toward the boxes "—are my files, likewise to be left alone. Out there—" he pointed toward the door through which she'd entered "—is the reception area, where you'll be working. Beyond that and down the hall—" this time he waved his hand, as if striving to indicate great distance "—there's a small washroom. It's near the door to the street, where you first came in."

That evidently concluded the tour, Audrey thought, because Mr. Wheeler didn't say anything more.

"Mind if I take a closer look at my desk?" she asked. "My telephone? My computer terminal?"

He must have misunderstood the question, because his expression became absolutely crestfallen, and he dropped his hands to his sides in a posture she could only describe as thoroughly defeated. "Didn't you see them when you first came in? Don't tell me Bruno took those, too. Hell, those were paid for."

"Who's Bruno?" she asked as she scrambled to follow Mr. Wheeler out of the office, thinking it was the only remark he'd made that she didn't quite understand.

Too late she realized he had halted only a few steps beyond the door, and, having hastened her step to catch up with him, she barreled into him at a pretty fast clip. Upon impact Mr. Wheeler went bolting forward, stumbling, landing on all fours on the floor. Audrey moved immediately to help him up, but she twisted her ankle just as she was reaching out to him and went hurtling forward herself. Before she knew what has happening, she had landed on his back, straddling him, perched the way a child might be when sitting astride a favorite uncle for a pony ride.

For one split second neither of them moved. Then Mr. Wheeler abruptly spun his body around, landed deftly on his fanny and caught Audrey capably in his lap. He narrowed his eyes at her, as if he wasn't quite sure what to make of a woman who would ride her boss like a horse. And as she met his gaze, Audrey's heart went *pitty-pat, pitty-pat, pitty-pat.* And then he smiled, a halfhearted little

smile that indicated he wasn't all that put off by their situation. After that, her heart went *zing-zing-zing-zing-zing*.

Oh, my.

He had caught her by the waist, and now his hands were
planted firmly atop each of her hips. Only then did Audrey
notice that his thumbs were idly grazing the bare skin revealed between her skirt and her top. Braving a glance
down, she realized that her clothing was too revealing for
mixed company given her new posture. Her skirt was hiked
up far enough on one side to reveal the lace of her red
panties through the hose beneath. Her sweater, too, was
riding high, though thankfully not high enough to under-
score the scant red brassiere beneath it.

Thinking back, she supposed she could have chosen
something a little less revealing for her first day on the job.
But the late-March morning had been surprisingly balmy,
and after months of cold, damp winter, she'd longed to feel
the warm breeze on as much of her body as she could.
Plus, she'd wanted to make a good impression on her new
boss. Plus, she'd really been in a red mood today.

Then again, there wasn't much in her wardrobe that
wasn't revealing. Having started off as a chunky kid, then
having bloomed into a chubby adolescent, Audrey had
worked and sweated for most of her adult years to drop her
weight. Now at twenty-eight years, five feet nine inches,
and 127 pounds, she liked to show herself off.

Hey, if you've got it, flaunt it, right? she'd thought. Especially if you didn't have much else going for you. Now,
however, she was beginning to think that maybe she
shouldn't have flaunted it quite so majorly in Mr. Wheeler's
direction.

As if he'd read her mind, he cleared his throat indeli-
cately, scattering her thoughts. But with her mind emptied,
her insides went all muddled and warm, because she realized he still had both hands around her naked waist. Even
more troubling, she had tangled her fingers in the crisp

white fabric of his shirt, and beneath her fingertips his heart fairly hummed with anticipation. As discreetly as she could, Audrey unwound the fingers of one hand and moved them to his shoulder. But that only brought into stark, raving focus the chiseled, well-defined musculature lurking beneath.

Simply put, her boss was built. And somehow she found herself wondering if maybe they couldn't just spend the rest of the day sitting in the middle of the floor this way, just exploring each other's bodies. Hey, it gave a whole new meaning to employee orientation.

"We, uh, we don't seem to be having a good day, do we?" he said softly, breaking the odd spell that had begun to descend around them.

Speak for yourself, Audrey thought. This had been the best day she'd had in a long, long time. However, she did concede, "I guess we're not really starting off as well as we could be."

He nodded at that but did nothing to alter their position on the floor. Instead, he only continued to gaze into her eyes as if he were looking for something very important there. A warmth spread through her that had nothing to do with the warble of the spring breeze rippling through the open door and everything to do with the gentle back-and-forth motion of her employer's thumbs across her bare skin.

Her employer. Oh, gosh. Oh, no. Oh, jeez.

Finally it registered on Audrey just how badly she had started off her first day on the job. With as much grace as she could manage, which, granted, under the circumstances wasn't much, she pushed herself up from her boss's lap. That, unfortunately, left her kneeling before him—pretty much the *second* worst position to be in with one's employer, right after riding him like a pony. Hurriedly she tugged her skirt back down around her thighs as best she could.

Mental note, Audrey, she told herself. *Shop for trousers. Big, loose trousers.*

Unfortunately such a purchase would have to wait until she had more money in her bank account. Or some money, for that matter, since $36.47 wasn't even enough to earn interest.

She shoved that thought away, too, and with only a marginally more graceful effort, managed to push herself up to standing. Mr. Wheeler, she noted, however, remained on the floor, and she hoped he wasn't trying to cop a peek up her skirt. Then again, she wondered, why would he bother after the free show she'd just given him?

Finally he rose, too, smoothing his hands down the front of his shirt once he was standing again. Somehow, though, Audrey got the feeling he performed the gesture not because his shirt was wrinkled, but because his palms were sweaty. Then, noting that she was suffering from that exact same malady herself, she gave her skirt one final tug, wiping her own hands dry in the bargain.

Only when they stood facing each other like two—relatively—normal human beings did her new employer speak again.

"Your desk," he said, throwing a hand to the left in a motion she supposed was meant to look nonchalant.

Audrey trained her gaze in the direction he indicated, noting again the cheap-looking piece of furniture accessorized by a chair that appeared to be far from comfortable. The computer terminal atop it was making some very dubious noises, as if it were on its last legs and just waiting for someone to push the right button that would put it out of its misery. She swung her attention back to her boss, not quite able to hide her astonishment at the appalling lack of amenities claimed by Rush Commercial Designs, Inc.

"That's it?" she asked. "You'll pardon me for asking, Mr. Wheeler, but—"

"Rush," he interrupted her.

"What?" she asked, confused.

"It's Mr. Rush, not Mr. Wheeler. Wheeler is my first name. Rush is my last name. Hence the name of the company being *Rush* Commercial Designs, Inc."

She thought about that for a moment. "Oh. Okay. Sorry."

"No problem."

"You'll pardon me for asking," she said again, "but shouldn't there be a little more to the office than, well...this?"

He nodded, the gesture clearly one of resignation. "Yes, there should be. But there's not. You've come to work for a failing business that I'm doing my damnedest to save, Miss Finnegan. My luck of late has been quite bad. I apologize for that, but I hope you're up to the task of working for someone who appears to be jinxed."

She straightened proudly, throwing her shoulders back, smiling as she smoothed a hand over the tuft of curls atop her head. "Don't you worry, Mr. Wheeler," she said, feeling confident for the first time in her entire life. "You and I should get along just fine. Because when it comes to bad luck, Audrey Finnegan wrote the book."

TWO

Wheeler assured himself during the week that followed that his initial introduction to Miss Audrey Finnegan must, without question, have been a fluke. No one, absolutely *no one*, could possibly be that inept, graceless and unfortunate. Her clumsiness had doubtless resulted from her being nervous about her first day on the job and nothing more. Once she caught on to the routine of his office, then everything would be okay.

Surely, on that first occasion, he told himself, Miss Finnegan had just been having One of Those Days. And surely, afterward, once she got the hang of things, a working relationship with her would ensue that, if not absolutely ideal, was certainly tolerable. That was what Wheeler told himself for the entirety of that first week.

Wheeler, however, was wrong.

Evidently, every day was One of Those Days when it came to Audrey Finnegan. And really, when he reflected back over those first five working days on this, the sixth working day, that first day with her had actually been her best to date. Because after one week of working with Miss Finnegan, Wheeler was fit to be tied. In a straitjacket. To a cement pylon. Near a very short pier.

As he strolled down Main Street toward his office the Monday after hiring his new—and thankfully temporary—secretary, he gradually slowed his pace and eyed his front door with *much* trepidation. In only five working days, the illustrious Miss Finnegan had managed to upstage every catastrophe that had befallen Wheeler in nine long months.

On Monday she crashed the office computer. Tuesday she trashed the office copier. Wednesday she bashed the office microwave. And Thursday she thrashed the office phone. On Friday, to top the week off, she wrecked her car. Or, rather, her friend's car, which she had borrowed for the day. Worse, she had wrecked it by slamming it into the back of Wheeler's car as they were leaving a nearby parking garage for the day. So now he was going to have to ride the bus to work for a while, until he could cough up the two-hundred-and-fifty-dollar deductible to have his car fixed.

And when Miss Finnegan hadn't been crashing, trashing, bashing and thrashing, she had been working at her desk, which *really* caused trouble. Simply put, Wheeler's new secretary had her own way of doing *everything,* and that way scarcely made sense to anyone other than Miss Finnegan.

At one point, when Wheeler asked her where she had filed the particulars for a design project he was bidding on for a local *minimart*—whose name began with the letter *W*—his new secretary retrieved it from where she had filed it under *L*. And when he had asked her what the letter *L* had to do with *design* or *minimart* or *W* for that matter, she had looked at him as if he were a complete moron, and then had explained to him, in a tone of voice that indicated she thought he was a complete moron, that *L* stood for *lottery.* Miss Finnegan, it would appear, always bought her lottery tickets at a minimart. Thus, it made sense—to her, at least—to file the plans in such a way.

And as for his new secretary's coffee... Well, suffice it to say that Wheeler *never* asked for a second cup. In fact, after that first day he'd pretty much foregone the first cup, too. He saw no reason to sample Miss Finnegan's coffee, unless, perhaps, he would have some reason to be awake for seven hundred hours straight.

Now as he pushed his troubling thoughts aside, he forced his feet to move forward again, carrying him through the brisk morning, past the other pedestrians hurrying to their respective places of business. No one else seemed to be too worried about what the day ahead held for them. No one else seemed to be frightened of what might greet *them* at *their* jobs. On the contrary, everyone *else* seemed to be remarkably bored by whatever might be going through *their* brains.

Then again, nobody else had to face the day ahead with Audrey Finnegan.

Oh, come on, Rush, he chastised himself as he quickened his step a bit. *It can't be as bad as you think. Miss Finnegan couldn't possibly be as horrific as you're recalling. You just had a rough week yourself, and you're looking to pin it on her. Be fair.*

That's what Wheeler told himself as he gripped the handle on the office door and inhaled a deep, fortifying breath before entering. Because he'd spent his weekend brooding over his ill fortune, he was naturally starting off his week now feeling more morose and defeated than the average person, and he wanted to blame someone other than himself. It was as simple as that.

So Miss Finnegan had taken out a couple of office machines, he recalled. So what? Wheeler had managed to undo whatever damage she had done, hadn't he? And sure, it had taken a big bite out of his day to act as computer repairman…and phone repairman…and copier repairman…and microwave repairman. But, seeing as how he hadn't had any real work to occupy his time anyway, that wasn't so bad, was it?

And, okay, so now his insurance company was canceling his policy because he was rear-ended by his secretary. He was probably going to have to sell his car soon, anyway, for the few thousand bucks it would bring in.

And, yeah, his files were in such a complete mess that he would probably *never* be able to figure them out for himself, should Miss Finnegan step in front of a bus and go to her final reward, which, considering the woman's luck, was not outside the realm of possibility.

There were worse things in life, right?

Right.

So chin up, he told himself further. Hey, after all, when things were this bad, they could only get better, couldn't they?

In spite of his little pep talk to himself, though, Wheeler felt anything but reassured when, very, very cautiously, he pushed the front door open. He hesitated a moment before entering, just to get a feel for things. No smell of smoke, he noted, heartening some. No strange sounds of mechanical upheaval. No power outages that he could readily discern…

Okay, so everything was fine, he realized with a long sigh of relief. See? He really had been overreacting when it came to memories of the previous week. Heartened some more, Wheeler strode into his outer office with all the confidence of a brass band, and found…

…chaos.

Truly. Chaos. What else could it be called when one's secretary had one's number-one client—the very, absolute last of one's reliable accounts—in a choke hold, clearly striving to throttle the life right out of the man? Because that was exactly what was happening. Audrey Finnegan

stood behind and had both arms wrapped resolutely around
the neck of Otis Denby, CEO of Denby Associates, and
Mr. Denby was turning blue as he fought for his very life.
He had gripped both hands around Miss Finnegan's fore-
arms, but she clearly had the upper hand, pumping his body
back and forth as she was with much abandon.

And all Wheeler could think was that he couldn't possibly allow her to murder Mr. Denby. Denby was, after all,
the only client Wheeler had left who paid his bills on time.

"Miss Finnegan!" he shouted at the top of his lungs as
he rushed forward. "What on *earth* do you think you're
doing?"

Without awaiting a response, he gripped her wrists
fiercely and yanked her hands free of his client's throat,
pushing her backward as he pulled the other man forward.
Immediately Mr. Denby curled one hand around his nape,
stretching his neck tight as he rolled his shoulders forward,
then back. His face and bald pate were red and mottled,
but he didn't seem to be struggling. Well, not *too* much,
anyway. His barrel chest rose and fell as he inhaled great
gulps of breath, and his pale blue eyes widened in what
could only be a combination of relief and terror.

And then, much to Wheeler's surprise, the other man
expelled a bark of delighted laughter. "Well I'll be
damned, Miss Finnegan," he said with a chuckle. "That
really did the trick. You're absolutely amazing. I never
would have suspected that a woman of your, uh…your attributes…could have such a gentle touch. Thank you."

Thank you? Wheeler echoed to himself. *Gentle touch?*
What the hell was going on here?

"What the hell is going on here?" he cried. He glanced
first at his client, then at Miss Finnegan, further demanding
an explanation.

She shrugged. "I worked for a chiropractor for a while,"
she said. She waved a hand negligently through the air.
"You pick up little things on your jobs. For example, ev-

erything I know about fashion accessories, I learned from just two weeks at The Limited.''

And speaking of fashion accessories, Wheeler noted through narrowed eyes that Miss Finnegan was in a blue mood today. Sapphire blue, to be specific. Her sapphire miniskirt was topped by a sapphire sweater that actually covered her hips. Sapphire hose ended in sapphire boots, and sapphire earrings swung from her ears. Her black hair, as always, was caught atop her head in a riot of curls, but even they seemed to be touched with blue.

Whatever she had learned about fashion during her time at The Limited, it must have been, well…limited. Because one thing he could definitely say about his temp—she was a color palate just waiting to happen. *If* she ever learned how to mix colors.

Wheeler pushed the thought away. ''Just what the devil is going on?'' he demanded again.

Before Miss Finnegan could add anything to her earlier explanation, Mr. Denby turned to him instead. ''Your new secretary just fixed a back problem I've had for decades, Rush. Decades. I can't tell you how much money I've spent on specialists over the years, only to have Miss Finnegan fix me up—'' he snapped his fingers merrily ''—like *that*.''

She shrugged again. ''My father suffered from the exact same thing,'' she said, sidestepping the accomplishment. ''You just have to know where to look, that's all.''

Where Wheeler decided to look was at the ceiling, while he tried not to think about the potential bodily damage his new secretary could have done to Mr. Denby. What on earth was he going to do with her? he wondered. Do with her that wasn't illegal, he meant.

''You should give her a raise, Rush,'' Denby suggested, answering that question, if none of the other numerous ones parading through his brain. ''Hell, I might just hire her away from you myself. She's delightful.''

When Wheeler looked down again, it was to find Miss

Finnegan blushing furiously and shaking a teasing finger—
one encased in what appeared to be a Scooby-Doo Band-
Aid—at Otis Denby. "Oh, now, Mr. Denby, that's very
sweet of you," she said. "But I couldn't possibly come to
work for you. My first commitment right now is to Mr.
Rush. It's not the One-Day-at-a-Timers' way to shirk our
responsibilities to our employers."

Shirk, Wheeler commanded her silently. *Please. By all
means. Shirk to your heart's content.*

But what he said was, "Mr. Denby, did we have an
appointment this morning?"

The other man shook his head. "I was in the neighborhood and thought I'd stop by." He glanced anxiously at
Miss Finnegan, then back at Wheeler. "Can we, uh…can
we speak privately, Rush?"

Here it comes, Wheeler thought with another sigh. The
big kiss-off. Otis Denby, his last, best client, was about to
take a powder. "Is that really necessary, sir?" he asked
halfheartedly.

Denby nodded fatalistically. "I'm afraid it is," he said.
"We're long overdue for this…uh…discussion."

Wheeler sighed heavily again before nodding, and was
about to open his mouth to accept defeat, when Miss Finnegan stepped in to interrupt him.

"Mr. Denby," she said, "do you by any chance know
anything about monopodial orchids?"

As questions went, it wasn't one Wheeler might have
expected from his secretary. Or anyone else on the planet,
for that matter. But Denby perked right up at the query.

"Why, yes, I do, Miss Finnegan. As a matter of fact,
growing orchids is an absolute passion of mine. That's
amazing that you'd share an interest like that, too."

She nodded. "Actually, it's more my mother's hobby
than my own, but I think it's more common than you realize," she assured him. Then she hurried on, "Before you
talk to Mr. Rush, do you mind if I ask you a few questions?

Mom is having such a hard time trying to figure out what she's doing wrong with her *Phalaenopsis*.''

Denby nodded sagely. ''Oh, those are tricky little bastards, aren't they?''

''Boy, you said it.''

He launched into what promised to be a very technical discussion about the plant in question, then, almost as an afterthought, turned to Wheeler. ''You don't mind, do you, Rush?'' he asked in a voice that pretty much answered his own question in the negative. ''This won't take but a minute.''

Wheeler nodded wearily. ''Don't worry about it, Mr. Denby. Just come into my office whenever you and Miss Finnegan are finished. My morning's pretty much clear.''

Hoo-boy, was that an understatement.

But Denby wasn't listening to Wheeler, because he had lost himself completely in his conversation with Miss Finnegan. She was pouring him a cup of her infamous coffee— as if Wheeler hadn't already done enough to terminate his business relationship with Otis Denby—and nodding at something the other man was saying, when Wheeler closed the door behind himself and made his way to the bar stool and drafting table that constituted what was left of his work station.

For some reason, he had the ''Death March'' stuck in his head, and he just couldn't shake it. Go figure. That didn't, however, prevent him from sitting down, making himself comfortable and pretending he had a really good idea as he stared at a blank piece of paper.

Oddly, though, he suddenly *did* have a really good idea. A remarkably good idea. A startlingly good idea. In fact, the more he thought about it, the more the idea grew. It was revolutionary, truly. The kind of idea he hadn't had for a very long time. And it would be just perfect for what Otis Denby was looking for in a commercial design.

Quickly, before the idea could escape, Wheeler gathered his pens and began to sketch.

What Denby had promised wouldn't take a minute, in fact, did not take a minute. It took about thirty minutes. But Wheeler scarcely noticed, because he spent the entire length of time sketching madly and enjoying a brainstorm that made Godzilla look like a cute little newt. And when that length of time finally had passed, it wasn't Denby who entered Wheeler's office—it was Miss Finnegan. She was humming under her breath an off-key rendition of what sounded like *The Flintstones* theme song, and carrying two cups of coffee, which, naturally, led Wheeler to believe that one of them was for him.

Damn.

Surprisingly, she only stumbled once as she entered, and even at that, she spilled just a few drops of coffee—merely enough to slightly enlarge two of the half-dozen or so coffee stains that had appeared on his rug over the past week. But he was still preoccupied by the last few drizzlings of his idea, so he barely registered the new stains. When she extended a cup toward him, he noticed that she had an ace bandage wound about her wrist. He was about to ask her what had happened when she spoke up, scattering his thoughts.

"Mr. Denby is a very nice man," she said.

Wheeler nodded dispassionately, curling his fingers around the coffee cup, which just went to show how suicidal he began to feel at the mention of his former client. "Yep. Denby's account was the best one I had. I'm hoping maybe this sketch I'm working on now will win him back."

"Had?" Miss Finnegan echoed. "Win him back? What are you talking about? He's still your client."

Wheeler glanced up, surprised. "He is?"

His secretary shrugged. "Sure."

"Then…why was he here this morning? Other than acting as your orchid mentor, I mean?"

She shrugged, clearly unconcerned by his worry. "He just needed to get a few things straightened out about the new design you're doing for him, that's all. Why did you think Mr. Denby wouldn't be your client anymore?"

He hesitated before answering. Naturally, it hadn't escaped his notice that Audrey Finnegan wasn't the most observant human being in the world. But surely even she could see how badly Rush Commercial Designs, Inc. was floundering. He had, after all, pretty much spelled it out for her that first day. And then there was that small matter of him having virtually no furniture, nor any clients. That seemed to him as if it would be kind of a dead giveaway. But then, that was Wheeler. Always assuming the obvious.

"Well," he began slowly, speaking his thoughts aloud, "there is that small matter of my having lost nearly every other client I have. I shouldn't think Mr. Denby would be too different in that respect."

"Oh, that," Miss Finnegan said as she sipped her coffee. Amazing. She didn't grimace once. "Mr. Denby is different, actually. And you didn't need those other clients, anyway."

Wheeler rather begged to differ, and didn't hesitate to tell her so. "Oh, I think, Miss Finnegan, that I did need those other clients. Desperately, in fact. I do have bills to pay." And lots of them, he recalled.

She wrinkled her nose as she shook her head, and Wheeler couldn't help but think, for some reason, that the gesture was really...very...well, *cute* came to mind.

"No, you didn't need them," she insisted lightly before enjoying—*enjoying*—another sip of her coffee.

"I didn't?"

She shook her head again. "Nah. They were alarmists."

"They were?"

This time she nodded. "Those kinds of people are ready to bail at the slightest sign of adversity. They have no staying power whatsoever. You would have lost them anyway, eventually.''

''I would?''

She offered him an expression that assured him he was dreaming if he thought otherwise. ''Oh, yeah. I've been going over your files as I've been rearranging them, and—''

Wheeler sat up straight at that, eyeing her in a panic. ''You…you've been rearranging my files?''

She enjoyed another unconcerned sip of coffee. ''Well, of course I've been rearranging your files. They were a mess—all alphabetical and everything. They made no sense at all. With all due respect to your former secretary, she could have learned a thing or two about filing.''

Wheeler closed his eyes. Rosalie, his former secretary, had been an absolute whiz at organizing his accounts. Although she wasn't the biggest people person on the planet—okay, so she'd been abrasive, gruff and borderline obnoxious—her filing system would have been the envy of the Pentagon and the IRS. His associates had always considered her a file Nazi, but Wheeler had been a bit more charitable, thinking her more of a file queen. No, scratch that. What Rosalie had been was a file goddess. And now Miss Finnegan, the pretender to the throne, had ''fixed'' those files.

Oh, no…

''Anyway,'' she went on, ''I've been trying to familiarize myself with your different clients, and, in my opinion at least, a lot of them were just fly-by-nights. I mean, I know you were starting up a new business, so you had to take whatever came your way, but some of these people, Mr. Rush…they just weren't the kind of clients you need. What you need to do is focus on attracting a more reliable, more stable account base.''

Wheeler narrowed his eyes at her. She sounded, almost,

like she knew what she was talking about. "How so?" he ventured.

She waved a negligent hand through the air. "Don't you worry about that," she said. "You just focus on your designs. I'll handle your accounts."

Oh, no, no, no, no, no. I don't *think* so. "Um, Miss Finnegan," he began, striving for a diplomacy he was nowhere close to feeling in his surging panic, "I appreciate your wanting to take some of the heat, but honestly, I think you should tell me what you're talking about."

She smiled, those luscious lips that he just couldn't quite ignore looking more tempting than ever. "Just trust me," she said mildly. "I know what I'm doing."

That, he thought, was open to debate. "But—"

"Is it okay if I take an extra half hour for lunch today?" she interrupted him. "I need to see about Marlene's car."

The change of subject nearly gave him mental whiplash. "No, before we talk about that, I think we need to talk about this other thing first."

She studied him in confusion. "What other thing?"

"This thing with my accounts," he prodded. "You're not suggesting that you—"

"I'll make the half hour up tomorrow," she said, still not quite grasping the topic he wanted to put first. "I'll only take thirty minutes for lunch, so it doesn't mess up the time thing."

"No, Miss Finnegan, before the time thing, back up to the other thing…the thing we were talking about a minute ago."

She squinted at him. "Were we talking about another thing a minute ago?" she asked. "What was it? I can't remember."

"*That* thing," he repeated emphatically. "That account thing. You know… That thing about how I should be attracting a more reliable account base. I want to talk about that."

She squinted some more. "Did I say something about an account thing?"

He nodded. Vigorously. And he battled the urge to start pulling his hair out by the roots. "Yes. You did. Or, at least, you started to. And it sounded like what you were going to say about the account thing was going to make sense and be very helpful. What was it?"

She thought for a long moment, putting her entire body into the effort. She shifted her weight to one foot, an action that thrust one rounded hip to the side—and hitched up her skirt in a manner that Wheeler simply could not ignore. And then she crossed one hand over her midsection, a gesture that thrust her plump breasts up even higher, in another manner that Wheeler simply could not ignore.

His secretary might not be the most graceful person on the planet when she moved, he thought, but when she was standing still like this, she had the most elegant lines he had ever seen on another human being. And when she started nibbling her lip with great concentration... Well. Suffice it to say that, even though he was eager to hear her take on his state of business affairs, Wheeler was in absolutely no hurry for her to finish up whatever she might be thinking about.

But after several minutes of contemplation, the only comment she offered was, "Huh. How about that? I don't remember what I was going to say."

Wheeler closed his eyes again, feeling his last drop of hope dry up. Ah, well. It had probably just been a fluke, anyway. Miss Finnegan didn't come across as too awfully savvy when it came to the business world. Without thinking, he lifted his coffee to his lips for an idle sip, and, as utter bitterness filled his mouth, he nearly choked to death.

Miss Finnegan immediately jumped to his rescue, which was unfortunate, because in doing so, she instinctively placed her own cup of coffee on his drafting table—his *tilted* drafting table—and the entire contents tipped over onto his truly revolutionary idea.

Wheeler watched with an almost detached feeling of defeat as what had promised to be the end of his worries was slowly obscured by a growing puddle of brown. And then, when his design was completely covered by the stain, the coffee, as if not quite finished ruining his life, spilled off the table and ran into his lap. Somehow the entire episode just seemed perfectly appropriate, and the only reaction he felt was one of vindication.

"Oh, no," Miss Finnegan groaned. "I can't believe I did that. Here, I can fix it. I swear I can."

Before he had a chance to object, she was fleeing his office, only to return within moments with a massive collection of paper towels. And although Wheeler's primary concern was for the design on his table, Miss Finnegan, evidently, was far more preoccupied by her concern for his lap. In any event, that was where she immediately focused her attentions.

And, my, but her attentions were…thorough. Nobody had ever gone after Wheeler's lap quite the way Audrey Finnegan did.

For a moment he was simply too stunned by her actions to do anything to stop them. Then, for another—longer, more delirious—moment, he found himself not really *wanting* to do anything to stop them. Thankfully, though, sanity stepped in, in that next moment, and somehow he gathered his wits enough to react. Quickly he reached for her hands to remove them from where they had settled, in a place on his upper thighs that was far too likely to rouse suspicion— among other things—should she venture any farther. Then, as gently as he could, he nudged her away.

"Thank you, Miss Finnegan," he said, "but I think you've done enough for one morning." Or one lifetime, for that matter, he thought further.

"I am so, so sorry," she told him.

Purely out of habit he replied, "No problem."

He turned his gaze to the design on which he'd spent the last thirty minutes and sighed heavily. He could salvage it—it was only a rough draft, after all, and the coffee had merely turned it brown, not obliterated it. That, however, wasn't the problem. The problem was that Miss Audrey Finnegan, with her clumsiness and gracelessness and appalling bad luck—even if she did have luscious lips and beautiful eyes and legs that wouldn't quit—was going to drive home what few nails were left in Wheeler's professional coffin. And she was going to do it in half the time it would take him to botch things himself.

He ought to let her go, he thought, strangely saddened by the realization. There really was no other way. He could call One-Day-at-a-Timers and make up some story about his and Miss Finnegan's incompatibility—he didn't want to get her into trouble, after all—and ask the temp agency to send someone else in her wake. At this point, anyone they sent would be an improvement.

But when he looked at her face and saw the abject apology and need for atonement in her expression, he couldn't quite form the words necessary to tell her she was fired. For all her awkwardness and misfortune, she really was very nice. And in spite of her having wrecked most of his office equipment—not to mention the first good idea he'd had in months—she had rather brightened up the place over the past week. Literally, he thought, when he recalled some of her outfits.

And then, of course, there was the small matter of her aforementioned luscious lips and beautiful eyes and legs that wouldn't quit, which he assured himself only marginally influenced his ultimate decision.

Wheeler sighed. He supposed it wouldn't kill him to give her a second chance. Surely they'd hit rock bottom by now. Things could only improve from here.

He ignored the little voice in the back of his brain that

reminded him how this was a conversation he'd had with himself pretty much daily since taking on Miss Finnegan. So, technically, she had already exhausted her second chances—more than once, in fact—and he had already watched things go from bad to worse—again, more than once.

Still, he did kind of like her. He didn't know why, but he did. Maybe because both of them seemed to be in the same boat—one that was fast sinking—where misfortune was concerned. Perhaps if he gave her just one more chance....

"Go ahead and take the extra half hour for lunch today," he said halfheartedly. "You can make it up tomorrow if you want."

Her eyes widened, making them appear even larger and greener than before—which was saying something. "O-okay," she replied, obviously confused by his reaction, but evidently unwilling to draw any more attention to her latest debacle than was absolutely necessary. "Um, thanks, Mr. Rush. For everything. I appreciate it."

He told himself he should ask her to call him Wheeler. Rush Designs, Inc. had never been a particularly formal business. Even when it was a successful one. He and his former secretary had been on a first-name basis from day one. Of course, Rosalie had been a fifty-six-year-old grand-mother of three, but that was beside the point. Still, there was no reason for him and Miss Finnegan to stand on ceremony.

Nevertheless, something prevented him from extending the invitation to call him by his first name, and he forced himself not to ask if he could call her by hers. He wasn't sure why. It just seemed best to keep their relationship as professional as possible. And even an insignificant, invisible barrier like the use of surnames would remind Wheeler that she was, first and foremost, his employee. He told him-

self it was essential that he keep that reminder planted
firmly in his brain.

In spite of that, when she smiled back at him, somewhere
deep inside him, in a place he'd never explored before, a
little bubble of heat went *fizz*. It was the oddest sensation
he'd ever felt. Before he had a chance to think about it,
though, Miss Finnegan spoke again.

"I am so sorry about the coffee," she repeated her earlier
apology. He had noted that first day her propensity for apologizing more than once. "I should have watched where I
was putting it. It was an accident, I swear. I really didn't
mean to—"

"Please, Miss Finnegan, don't worry about it," he said,
interrupting her. "Let's just both make a pact to be more
careful from here on out, all right? And then let's just forget
it ever happened."

She nodded vigorously. "Okay. I will if you will. And
I promise you that nothing like that will happen again.
Ever. I won't let you down, Mr. Rush. I can assure you of
that. From here on out, with you and me working together,
Rush Commercial Designs, Inc., is headed for great, great
things."

Three

Audrey approached her second Tuesday on the job with an air of caution, which was perfectly understandable, all things considered. She told herself that the previous week had been her warm-up, that anything that had gone wrong during those first five days could be excused as new-job jitters or getting a feel for things or just not being familiar with her new surroundings. But by week two, she thought, things really should start to level off. So, naturally she was very much looking forward to surviving, er, rather, enjoying it.

And in some ways, by that second day of week two, things were already starting to level off—hey, that coffee-spilling incident of the day before could have happened to anybody. In spite of her lack of skills where machinery was concerned—and she worked on those by simply avoiding what office machinery she could—Audrey had people capabilities that were way above average.

So she had focused on those talents instead, had spent

much of her time last week contacting what was left of Mr.
Rush's client base to update their files and put a few feelers
out as to what they were looking for in a design company.
She told herself that was probably something her employer
would want to do himself, but he had so many other things
on his mind, the last thing Audrey wanted to do was make
him rehash everything for her.

So she had spoken to his clients herself, to find out what
kind of people and businesses they were and what they
were looking for in a commercial design company, had
chatted amiably about life in general, and had reassured
them that Rush Commercial Designs, Inc., was well into
recovery and going like gangbusters. As a result, she'd
started feeling a little bit like she was a part of the company
herself.

And she'd discovered pretty quickly what a nice feeling
that was. None of her other jobs had ever made her feel
like she was contributing much of anything. None of them
had made her feel as if she were necessary. But Mr. Rush
was a man in obvious need of help, and Audrey was, by
nature, a very helpful person. Plus, when it came to being
down on your luck, she knew all the right moves. She was
confident, if of nothing else, that she could make a difference here.

And even after only one week of trying, she was already
feeling as if she had.

"Good morning, Miss Finnegan."

She glanced up from her desk to see Mr. Rush striding
through the door, carrying, as he was every morning, a huge
cup of coffee, which she just couldn't understand, because
she always had a fresh pot waiting for him when he came
in.

"Good morning, Mr. Rush," she replied cheerily.
"Good to see you made it in before the rain."

He arched his eyebrows in surprise. "Is it supposed to
rain today?"

She gaped at him. "Didn't you notice the black clouds? The Weather Channel says it's going to be a real doozy. There's even a tornado watch."

He arched his eyebrows in obvious surprise. "No kidding?"

Boy, did he need looking after, Audrey thought with a slow shake of her head. How on earth had he made it this far in life all by himself?

"Fortunately," she told him, "you don't have anything scheduled outside the office, so you can stay nice and dry inside."

He looked crestfallen at the news. "Yes, well, that scarcely comes as a surprise, does it?"

"I don't know, does it?"

He expelled a soft sound of distress. "Miss Finnegan, please. You don't have to pretend. I know the business is on its last legs, and it's only a matter of time before the last of my clients has pulled out on me. So you don't—"

"Actually, you picked up a couple of new clients last week," she reminded him.

"I know," he conceded, "but they're not exactly huge corporations bulging with expendable income, are they? The projects they've commissioned will barely cover the month's utility bills."

"They're brand-new businesses," she pointed out, "starting on the ground floor. You have the opportunity to send them sky-high. And just think how grateful they'll be to you when you do. Someday they'll be huge, prosperous companies, and they'll be indebted to you."

He narrowed his eyes at her, as if he hadn't thought about it like that. "I suppose you're right," he said. "In any event, they've paid me money to do work for them, haven't they? So I'll do my best by them."

He started toward his office, then hesitated, slowing his pace until he had stopped completely in his tracks. For one long moment he only stood there, gazing blindly at a blank spot on the wall. Audrey didn't say anything to disturb him, as he seemed to have his mind fixed intently on something very important that had nothing to do with the nice shade of mauve there. When he turned to look at her, he was smiling, a tentative, secretive little smile that she found *very* becoming.

"Hold my calls this morning, will you, Miss Finnegan?" he asked quietly, in a voice that told her he was still quite preoccupied. "I think I have an idea for the new Windsor Deli account." He nodded slowly, then began to walk toward his office again. "Yeah, I do," he muttered triumphantly. But he didn't seem to be talking to Audrey. "I have a really, really *good* idea."

When he disappeared into his office and closed the door behind him, she smiled with much satisfaction. See? He really did need her. Even if it was just to be a reassuring presence in his life.

She turned in her chair and eyed the computer terminal on her desk with as much confidence as she could muster. Then, after pushing up the sleeves of her fuchsia sweater, she doubled her fists and held them aloft like a prizefighter.

"Okay," she said to the machine. "You and me, we're going to have a little session. I'm going to type some letters, and you're going to let me do it without beeping or booping or going blank on me. Got it?"

The cursor blinked at her benignly, but the computer uttered not a sound. She nodded victoriously. "Good," she said.

And, humming "You Were Meant for Me" under her breath, Audrey went to work.

It was amazing, really, Wheeler thought some hours later, what you could do with the germ of an idea. As he gazed at the project on his work table, he smiled with much satisfaction. Damn, he was good. He'd forgotten just how good, over the past few months. He remembered now why he'd gone into this line of work to begin with. Because it was interesting. Because it was fun. Because it was what he did best.

He was coming out of his slump now—he could feel it. He didn't know why or how it had come about, but Rush Commercial Designs, Inc. was about to undergo an upswing. A *major* upswing. He could feel it. Somehow, he just *knew* he was on the road to recovery. The two new accounts that had come about last week, even if they were meager, were just the beginning. Best of all, his creativity was back. His brain was functioning again. His talent and skills hadn't packed up and abandoned him, after all. And now he was ready to recoup the losses he'd suffered.

As if inspired by his optimism, there was a soft rap at Wheeler's office door that sounded remarkably like opportunity knocking. He smiled at the very idea.

"Yes, Miss Finnegan?" he called out.

The door opened slowly, as if she were being extra careful not to create some debacle that would blow it off its hinges. Thankfully all that happened was that the door got stuck on a bump in the carpet, so she had to shove it a few times—real hard—to get it to open. Unfortunately she wound up putting a bit more effort into her final push than was actually necessary, because the door gave just as her shoulder made contact, an action that resulted in her barreling over the threshold at an alarming speed.

Fortunately—a wild occurrence for her—she recovered herself before she went sprawling onto her knees or into Wheeler—so she ended up only looking a little foolish, and *not* doing anyone any bodily harm. The bright spots of pink that appeared on her cheeks were almost exactly the same hue as the bright fuchsia outfit she wore—from neck to toe—and he marveled again that when it came to her wardrobe, she was just so terribly…uh…monochromatic. Still, there was a lot to be said for a woman in a hot-pink dress.

"Sorry," she mumbled after she'd righted herself.

"No problem," Wheeler replied automatically.

It was, after all, an exchange the two of them shared at least a dozen times daily since her arrival at the office.

"What was it you wanted, Miss Finnegan?"

"Oh. There's a Mr. Bernardi on the phone," she said. "I would have buzzed you on the intercom, but I sort of broke it. Again." She blushed once more, then hurried on, "But this Mr. Bernardi...?"

Wheeler narrowed his eyes at the announcement, recognizing the name—who in Louisville wouldn't?—but certain his optimism had overtaken his good sense. "Not Charles Bernardi? The CEO of Bernardi Electronics?" he asked, knowing he was foolish to feel so hopeful. It was probably Joe Bernardi, bill collector, leaving a threatening message.

But when Miss Finnegan brightened, Wheeler knew his first assumption must be correct. "Yeah, that's him," she said. "He's a really nice man. His mother and my mother are both in the same bunco club—can you imagine the coincidence?"

"*You* know Charles Bernardi?" he asked, incredulous. There was no way she could be traveling in the same social circle as Louisville's foremost businessman and rumored billionaire.

She shook her head. "Oh, gosh, no. At least, I didn't until a few minutes ago. But he's very easy to talk to."

Now Wheeler squeezed his eyes shut. His temp had been out there chatting up Charles Bernardi? Oh, great. So much for hoping for *that* account.

"Anyway," she said, "he wants to talk to you. You were recommended by the owner of Windsor Deli, who just happens to be Mr. Bernardi's daughter."

"No way," Wheeler said.

She nodded, smiling. "Big way. So you might want to take the call."

She didn't have to tell him twice. Wheeler fairly leaped from his seat and snatched up the telephone.

Twenty minutes later, he had made an appointment to offer a presentation to the biggest employer in town, one that, should he land the account—and even after only twenty minutes on the phone with Charles Bernardi, he was fairly confident he *would* land the account—would pull his business right up from the bottom of the heap.

And for some reason, all he could think was that Miss Finnegan was somehow partly responsible. He had no idea why such an idea had landed in his head, but it was a feeling he just couldn't shake. Funny, but ever since he'd taken her on last week, he'd gradually begun to pull out of his slump. He'd had a couple of very good ideas, had signed a handful of new accounts and looked to be *this close* to closing another, one that would be an absolute lifesaver. Or, at least, a business saver. This was definitely the beginning of good things for Wheeler.

Huh. How about that? he thought. Miss Audrey Finnegan, with all her ill fortune, was turning out to be quite the good-luck charm for him.

Wheeler smiled at the thought. Nah. That was going a bit too far. There was no way a woman like that, with whom bad luck walked hand in hand, could ever be a lucky talisman for anyone. Still, the morning's events called for a celebration of sorts. So he rose and made his way to the outer office, where he found his secretary muttering something that sounded marginally profane under her breath at the computer.

"Miss Finnegan," he said.

She jumped at the sound of his voice, spinning around so quickly in her chair that she almost tumbled right out of it. Thankfully, at the last minute, she grabbed the side of her desk and managed—just barely—to stay seated.

"I just made an appointment that's likely to land me the biggest account of my entire career. Would you care to join me for a celebratory lunch at Kunz's?" He gestured toward the front door, through which blinding sunlight spilled. "It would appear that the rain has decided not to make an appearance after all. It's turned out to be a beautiful day—in more ways than one."

She smiled at his offer, and something warm and mushy squooshed through Wheeler's belly at the sight of it. Strange, that. He'd never felt anything go squooshing through him before. It was kind of an enjoyable sensation. Unable to help himself, he grinned back at her in return.

"Oh, you bet, Mr. Rush," she said. "Congratulations on a job well done."

"Congratulations right back at you, Miss Finnegan. Something tells me this was a team effort."

Her smile then suddenly became shy, and those two spots of pink reappeared on her cheeks. "Oh, thank you, but it was all your doing. I only work here."

He chuckled low. "Well. At any rate, you've proved to be a nice addition to the business," he said.

She blushed even more furiously at his innocently offered compliment, and the warm, mushy feeling in his stomach compounded. "I'll just get my purse," she told him, "and we can go."

It was a bad idea, lunch. Wheeler realized belatedly that he should have kept in mind exactly what kind of woman his secretary was—namely, jinxed to the max. Between her spilling her iced tea into *her* lap, and then dumping his salad into *his* lap when she jumped up at the impact, they both left the restaurant prematurely, before their lunches even arrived. They also left the restaurant stained. And wet. And uncomfortable.

Miss Finnegan, he noted, strode back to the office with her oversize—and very pink—purse placed strategically over the wet stain on her skirt. He, however, didn't have the luxury of fashion accessories, so he was forced to make the five-block walk with a big ol' vinaigrette stain dead center on his trousers. It was, in a word, unpleasant.

But his worry became immaterial within two blocks of the restaurant, anyway, because out of nowhere the blue skies blackened, and the promised rain arrived—in spades. By the time they arrived back at the Rush Commercial Designs, Inc. offices, having battled both surly traffic and tsunami conditions, both were wringing wet, chilled to the bone and feeling in no way celebratory.

"I'm sorry," Miss Finnegan apologized as they pushed through the front door. "I am really, really sorry."

Wheeler shoved both hands through his wet hair, slicking it back from his forehead. In spite of his irritation at getting caught out in the rain that way, he couldn't help but feel sorry for Miss Finnegan. After all, he had a spare change of clothes in his office, of which he intended to make use posthaste. She, however, was going to be stuck for the rest of the day in those soaking wet clothes that clung to her like a second skin, outlining every salient curve she possessed as if she were wearing nothing at all, and...

His thoughts got stuck right there, because he noted just how accurately he had been taking in the sight of his secretary. Her hot-pink outfit was still hot-pink, but where before it had been snug, now it was...it was...well, it was just plain hot. Thankfully she was wearing underwear beneath it.

Then it occurred to Wheeler that the only way he could possibly know that she was wearing underwear beneath it was because he could see the garments perfectly delineated under her wet clothing. And it occurred to him *then* that what Miss Finnegan wore under her clothes was every bit as skimpy as her clothing itself. The twin globes of her breasts—and ample they were, too—plumped out of the top of her brassiere, and her bikini panties—her *thong* panties, he noted further, reluctantly, he told himself, when she spun around—were nearly nonexistent.

And he realized then that he wouldn't be the one wearing his spare clothing for the rest of the day. Miss Finnegan would be. Otherwise, there was no way he would get anything done. Well, anything other than some serious—and completely inappropriate for an office climate—daydreaming.

He hastened toward his office, explaining about the change of clothes as he went, retrieving the shirt and trousers as quickly as he could, shoving them into Miss Finnegan's hands and escorting her, quite forcibly now, into his office so that she could change, all the while prattling on and on about God only knew what, anything to keep his mind off her body. Her wet, round, rosy, wet, uh— Anything to keep his mind off her plight.

"Are you sure?" she called from the other side when he had, with much relief, closed the door behind her. "I don't want to take your only change of clothes."

"Absolutely, I'm sure," he replied, gripping the knob violently so that he wouldn't, oh, say…submit to the hormonal surge he was experiencing, turn the knob and open the door and stumble upon her half-naked. "By all means. It would be downright unchivalrous of me to change into warm, dry clothes and leave you out here in your wet, clingy, revealing, luscious, uh—" He slapped a hand over his mouth before he could say anything stupid. Well, stupid*er,* he amended.

"That's awfully nice of you, Mr. Rush."

"Don't mention it," he told her.

"You are very chivalrous," she added through the door, her voice sounding softer somehow than it had before. "And I really am very sorry about the rain."

"Why are you apologizing?" he asked, puzzled. "It's not your fault the weather turned nasty."

He heard something wet fall to the floor on the other side of the door and squeezed his eyes shut to fend off the licentious imagery he knew would follow. Unfortunately, closing his eyes only made the image that much more graphic, so he snapped his eyes open again.

But all he could think about was the fact that Miss Finnegan was standing in his office with her wet things on the floor, probably naked by now, and readying herself to put on his clothing without a stitch of her own garments underneath. And then, it hit him like a ton of wet thong bikini panties, that he wanted very badly to go in there and get naked with her.

How very, very troubling.

"I feel like the rain is my fault," she said, intruding on Wheeler's thoughts from the other side of the door, which he was now clasping with a white-knuckled grip.

He shook off his salacious ideas as best he could. "Why would you feel like that's your fault?" he asked again, mystified.

Another wet thump from the other side of the door had his mind spinning out of control again, until her voice pulled him back. "Well, you may not have noticed this," she began softly, slowly, "but I'm sort of…unlucky."

Wheeler feigned shock as best he could. "No. You don't say."

"It's true, I'm afraid. All the Finnegans, from my great-grandmother Fiona on down, have been cursed from the day they were born."

Again, Wheeler strove for astonishment, hoping he wasn't laying it on too thick, as he said, "Get out."

She opened his office door then, but had to wrestle it out of Wheeler's death grip to do so. And although he would have sworn there was no way Miss Finnegan could have possibly tested his hormonal restraint any more than she had when she'd been soaking wet, he realized, belatedly, that dressed in men's clothing, she was even more tempting.

And not just any men's clothing, either. But Wheeler's. Never had his run-of-the-mill white dress shirts and dark trousers looked better than they did hugging Miss Finnegan's shapely curves. She'd even cinched his black leather belt tightly around her waist and donned his necktie, looping the length of brightly colored silk—his neckties were Wheeler's one concession to whimsy—into an expert Windsor knot at her throat.

She looked—he hated to say it—delectable. And it was only with a Herculean effort that he kept his gaze from lingering below her neck.

"I'm really surprised you haven't noticed," she said doubtfully in response to his assurance that he hadn't noticed her rather dubious luck. "I mean, I always thought it was kind of obvious myself. Most people notice it right off the bat."

What Wheeler noticed when he returned his gaze to her face was how lush her mouth was, how green her eyes were, and how, even wet, the mop of curls atop her head fairly danced with every movement she made.

"Well," he said. "I've, uh…I've had a lot on my mind lately. I may have noticed once or twice that you, um…you, uh…"

"Have a lot of accidents?" she supplied helpfully.

"Well, okay, yes, I did notice that," he conceded.

"I also tend to lose things a lot," she added.

"Lose things?" he echoed. "Like what?"

She shrugged. "Like car keys. Contact lenses. Jobs. Boyfriends. That kind of thing."

"Oh."

"And then there's that small matter of my sort of, oh…totally ruining things for other people."

That caught Wheeler's interest. In a big way. "Ruining things? How so?"

She passed by him on a rush of honeysuckle-scented air, close enough so that Wheeler could feel her heat. Or perhaps he just imagined that. In any case, he liked it.

"Oh, just little things," she said, spinning back around

to face him. "Like how my friend Marlene's plumbing and furnace went out right after I moved in with her. And how, right after I started dating him, Brad—he's my latest ex-boyfriend—became sort of, um…impotent?"

This time Wheeler was the one to battle a blush. He really didn't want to hear this.

Unfortunately Miss Finnegan seemed intent on telling him all about it. "Not that we ever…you know. I have to know a guy really, really well before I…you know…with him. And Brad and I only dated two months, so any…you know…was totally out of the question. But still. He basically told me in no uncertain terms that we would never…you know…because he just couldn't…you know…where I was concerned. So I felt really bad about that, even though I didn't really want to…you know…with him anyway."

Strangely Wheeler followed every word of her story. But before he could comment, she rushed on to another one.

"And then there was that time when I was in Girl Scouts? Well, suffice it to say that Camp Whanahini never quite recovered from that flood."

Now, that, Wheeler thought, was simply going too far. "Miss Finnegan, you can't possibly think that you were responsible for a flood."

She gazed back at him blankly, as if he'd just said something incredibly stupid. "You don't think so?"

"Of course not."

"Then what about that freak snowstorm a few years ago that practically shut down the entire state? That happened right after I moved here."

"Oh, please. Next you'll be telling me you're responsible for the April third tornadoes that devastated the city twenty-odd years ago."

She nibbled her lip anxiously. "Well…actually…I was sort of visiting cousins here at the time."

Wheeler shook his head. Okay, she was definitely one of

those people to whom bad luck seemed to cling. But to blame herself for all manner of natural disaster? That was pushing it a bit, even where Audrey Finnegan was concerned.

"Miss Finnegan—"

But she cut him off before he could finish. "Mr. Wheeler, just accept my apology, okay? And know that I'll do my best not to infect you with my bad luck."

He smiled at that. "On the contrary, Miss Finnegan, you seem to have brought me nothing but *good* luck since your arrival."

Her expression told him just how doubtful she was about that. "What do you mean?"

"I mean, think about it. Since you came to work for me, I've avoided losing any more accounts and have signed some new ones. I have a meeting with Charles Bernardi that looks to be *very* promising. And that's an account that any other commercial designer in Louisville would kill to get, one that could easily float my entire business for the next few years. That's not what I'd call bad luck. Looks to me like you're the best kind of good-luck charm."

"But all those coffee stains on your carpet, and losing your lunch today, and—"

"Stains I can handle, Miss Finnegan. It's the business that's most important. And that's picking up speed like it never has before." He chuckled happily, surprised to realize that he truly didn't mind all the mishaps. "You're my good-luck charm. That's all there is to it."

Oddly, although he uttered those reassurances only as platitudes meant to make her feel better, Wheeler found himself halfway believing them. Maybe she really was his good-luck charm. Stranger things had happened.

For a moment Miss Finnegan only gazed at him as if he'd lost his mind. Then slowly, very slowly, she began to smile back. "I guess it's possible," she said. Then, glancing quickly down at the shirt whose sleeves were rolled to her elbows, she murmured, "Thanks, Mr. Rush. For the change of clothes, I mean. I'll take good care of them. I hung my wet stuff on your coatrack. I hope that was okay."

"Don't worry about it, Miss Finnegan," he told her. "That will be fine."

And somehow, at that moment, Wheeler was quite certain that his luck really had changed. His business was on the road to recovery. His creativity had been restored. And now he could spend the rest of the day gazing at hot pink underwear dangling from his coatrack. Good luck, indeed, all around.

And it had all begun, strangely enough, with the arrival of Audrey Finnegan in his life.

Four

By the end of that second week on the job, Audrey really did hit her stride, and everything wound up going like clockwork. Okay, going like clockwork that didn't exactly tell the correct time, but still…things ended up *much* better than they had that first week.

She figured out the phone system—pretty much. She opened up every file on the computer with absolutely no help from Mr. Rush—well, *almost* absolutely no help from him. She color-coded the entire filing system in a way that made perfect sense—even if her boss couldn't quite grasp what that sense was. And she worked her way up to a fifty-percent success rate with the microwave popcorn.

Best of all, though, she only broke one thing in the whole, entire office. One little, teensy, infinitesimal, itty-bitty thing. Okay, so it was Mr. Rush's lucky mechanical pencil that his great-grandfather had given him the day he'd earned his master's degree in business. It was still really little, even if it was solid gold. And hey, he shouldn't have left it lying around where she might step on it. Anybody could have snapped it in two like that when they were standing on his desk to change a lightbulb. Sheesh.

All in all, things were looking way, way up in Audrey's life, to the point where she hardly ever even thought about what a cursed family she'd been born into. In addition to her new job, she'd found a new place to live—right on the bus line, so she didn't have to worry about going carless—and it *wasn't* a basement apartment. On the contrary, she moved into a nice, albeit little, studio on the top floor of a big Victorian in the Highlands, complete with a turret room that made a great place for her bed. And if all the major appliances were kind of moody—or not working... whatever—well, that was just one of those little sacrifices you had to make, right?

Best of all, Audrey's daily calls to the Humane Society had panned out, because her cat, Roxanne, had turned up there. And when she had gone to pick her up, she'd even adopted Roxanne's cage mate, Marco, a grumpy Siamese to whom her silver tabby had taken a great liking for some reason.

Still, she knew better than to think that this wave of seeming good fortune would last. Every now and then throughout her life, Audrey had experienced these temporary pockets of luck where it would appear that she was on her way to good things. Naturally, though, these temporary pockets were just, well, temporary. So she didn't get her hopes up that this was the beginning of great things, and she prepared herself for the backlash that was bound to come eventually.

Because there would be a backlash—of that she was absolutely certain. All good things—and in Audrey's case, all good luck—must come to an end, and she knew better than to be lulled into a false sense of security, just because things were going well for a change. Still, that didn't mean

she couldn't enjoy this leveling-off period for as long as it
lasted, right? She might as well make the most of it.

Besides, it wasn't like *everything* was suddenly going
right. She still felt the absence in her life of a boyfriend,
someone with whom to share the good times, however temporary. It would be nice, for example, she thought as she
pulled a chicken pot pie out of her oven Saturday night, to
celebrate her new apartment with a nice, warm, cute body,
especially one with warm, chocolate-brown eyes to just curl
up and die for. But, hey, guys were a dime a dozen, weren't
they? Something would turn up eventually. No biggie.

A faint, damp breeze blew in the window over her sink,
bringing with it the kiss of cool spring rain. In response
she turned her gaze out the window, seeing on the opposite
side of the street below a couple huddled beneath a wide
umbrella, sharing a kiss, a cuddle and a couple of laughs.
Something inside Audrey twisted sadly at the sight, and she
focused her attention once again on her dinner, trying to
push thoughts of her single status out of her head.

To no avail.

She tried to tell herself that, considering the luck—or
lack thereof—she'd had with men, she was probably much
better off without a boyfriend, anyway. After all, she had
Roxanne and Marco to keep her company, she reminded
herself, and her new boss more than filled up any romantic
fantasies she might have. Even if fantasies of romance were
all she would be getting where her employer was concerned. They'd be enough. They were really good fantasies.

Not that she was falling in love with Mr. Rush—no, no.
Maybe a little crush, she conceded, but love? No way. Although he was really cute and sweet and funny and everything, it would be pointless to try to develop anything more
than a working relationship with him. Audrey was his temp,
after all. And temp, by definition, meant temporary.
Granted, she was only obligated to be temporary in a professional sense, but the very basis of her relationship with

the guy was no-strings-attached, and she would do well to remember that.

Because in no way had he indicated he had any desire to attach strings to her. Not that she wanted to be tied to some guy, anyway. Not even a guy like Wheeler Rush. And not just because, as in every other aspect of her life, she was unlucky in love, either. But because she hadn't been lying to him when she said her bad luck always seemed to infect the people with whom she became involved.

The Finnegan history of misfortune was a long and rich one, full of episodes where the Finnegans had unwittingly dragged down their unsuspecting loved ones. And Audrey really didn't want to see Mr. Rush suffering from any more bad luck than he'd already had lately. There was only so much a man could take, after all.

She just didn't like living alone, that was her problem. She was socially gregarious by nature, and it had been fun shacking up with Marlene, even if she and her best friend didn't get along all that well. But Marlene had made it clear that Audrey was starting to cramp her style. Not to mention her bathroom. So Audrey knew she was better off now having found a place of her own. What difference did it make if she had to be alone?

And why was she having this conversation with herself, anyway? she wondered as she set the pot pie on her kitchen table, gathered up a fat paperback and sat down to read. This was all immaterial. She wasn't alone. She had her cats—there they were, right there. Roxanne and Marco gazed at her from the windowsill where they lay beside each other, their expressions bored, as if they really couldn't care less that she was having chicken pot pie for supper and they weren't.

"You wish," she told the cats as she lifted a healthy spoonful to her mouth. After swallowing, she told them, "You can't have this. It's way too much cholesterol for you guys. Besides, you're having seafood tonight. Tuna-whitefish buffet. You'll love it.''

They didn't look convinced.

"Really," she told them, digging in for another bite. "Trust me."

The sound of her door buzzer surprised her, halting just shy of her mouth the generous bite she had been about to inhale. She wasn't expecting anyone on a Saturday evening, and she was dressed for exactly that occasion—no makeup, hair spilling in loose curls from a long ponytail that wouldn't quite stay bound. She wore baggy black sweat-pants and an oversize T-shirt that read Yes, But Not the Inclination, and padded to the front door in big athletic socks that completed her ensemble.

Cautiously she gazed through the peephole, squinting to make out the indistinct blur that stood on the other side. To say she was surprised to realize that it was her boss would have been an understatement. But what was truly amazing was that he appeared to be holding a big bouquet of flowers in one hand and a wrapped gift in the other. All Audrey could think was that he must be on his way some-where else and that he'd just dropped by her new apartment because…because…

Well, maybe he got lost.

Quickly she loosed the chain and spun the dead bolt, then carefully tugged the door inward. "Hi, Mr. Rush," she greeted him, hoping her astonishment at his appearance didn't show in her voice.

He opened his mouth to respond, but no words came out. Instead, he only widened his eyes for a moment, then dropped his gaze to her toes and gradually worked his way back up to her face. Then he blinked three times in rapid succession, as if she'd turned into a puff of smoke and disappeared before his very eyes.

"Miss Finnegan?" he asked softly, his voice touched with incredulity.

She nodded. "Uh-huh. Hi, Mr. Rush. What are you doing here?"

"I... *Miss Finnegan?*"

She nodded again. "Yeah?"

He shook his head hard, as if to clear it, then smiled. "I'm sorry. I almost didn't recognize you. You look..."

His voice trailed off before he completed the observation, and she thanked her unlucky stars for that. The last thing she needed to hear was how icky she looked in her spare time. But this was her day off, she reminded herself, a day she'd spent moving into her new digs. Why would she go to all the trouble to look presentable just for a bunch of boxes she was unpacking and the furniture she was rearranging?

In spite of the realization that she was perfectly within her rights to look like a bum in the privacy of her own home, Audrey quickly smoothed a hand back over her hair and tugged down her T-shirt with all the imperiousness of a queen.

And, telling herself she did *not* sound apologetic when she did it, she said softly, "Well, it *is* my day off. And I wasn't expecting company. And I've been moving. And—"

He chuckled low, and again she got the feeling his reaction was spurred by disbelief. "No, I didn't mean that. I meant...you look..."

But again he stopped before completing whatever he'd been about to say. Instead he only continued to gaze at her in silence, almost studying her, really, the ghost of a smile playing about his lips.

"Do you want to come in?" she asked, torn between hoping against hope that he accepted her invitation, and desperately wishing he would decline it.

Her question seemed to snap him out of his reverie— well, kind of. He smiled warmly as he said, "Yes, please. I'd like that very much."

She opened the door wider to allow him entrance, inhaling deeply as he strode by her, noting, as always—and enjoying, as always—the mix of musk and mint and man that she had come to associate with him. Tonight, he had dressed more casually than he did for work, having bypassed his traditional trousers, dress shirt and tie in favor of faded blue jeans and a tobacco-colored sweater that complemented his brown eyes just so very nicely.

Audrey bit back a sigh as he came to a stop at the archway between her kitchen and living area—to call it a living *room* would have been far too generous—then spun around to look at her. Gosh, he was handsome. Good thing she wasn't falling in love with him.

"Nice place," he said.

He should know, she thought. From where he stood, he could see every last inch of it.

"It's small," she pointed out unnecessarily.

He shrugged the comment off. "It's no smaller than my place. And you've got everything you need."

That was true, she thought. Now that he was here.

"Yesterday," he went on, scattering her thoughts, "when you told me where your new apartment was, it didn't register right away. Then today it hit me. You're practically right around the corner from me."

She smiled, genuinely delighted to hear about the coincidence. "Really?"

He nodded. "I'm over on Hepburn."

That was only two blocks. "No kidding," she said. "That's amazing. Great minds think alike, huh?"

He smiled back. "More like shrinking wallets necessitate similar circumstances," he corrected her. "Anyway," he hurried on, "I just wanted to drop by and say happy housewarming." He extended both the flowers and the gift toward her.

"For me?" she asked, again surprised and delighted by the developments.

"It isn't much," he told her quickly. "Just a little something to say welcome to the neighborhood."

Hey, it could be nothing but a boxful of buffalo chips, and Audrey would still be charmed by it. It was, after all, a gift from Mr. Rush. "Can I open it now?" she asked.

She wasn't sure, but she thought he blushed a little bit at her question. "Ah, yeah…yeah, sure," he stammered. "If you want to."

Of course she wanted to. She crossed the kitchen to retrieve the gifts from him, setting the gaily wrapped package on the table while she went in search of an appropriate receptacle for the flowers. But naturally she had nothing appropriate for such a beautiful collection of daisies and carnations and baby's breath. She finally settled for a hurricane glass her mother had brought her as a souvenir of Pat O'Brian's in New Orleans.

"They're beautiful," she told him as she hastily arranged the flowers and added water. Then she set them at the center of the kitchen table and took a step back to admire them. "They're just what the place needed to brighten it up." Well, those and a certain brown-eyed boss of her acquaintance, she amended silently. But there was no reason she had to tell him that.

He must have noticed the remnants of her supper then, because he pointed at her chicken pot pie and said, "I'm sorry—I interrupted your dinner, didn't I?"

She chuckled. "Yeah, well, the word *dinner* is pushing it, I think. Like I said, I've spent the day unpacking and—"

"I should have called first," he said.

"No," she assured him. "No, that's okay. Honest. I like surprises. I do. Besides, the phone's not hooked up yet." Nor would it be, until she could scrounge up the deposit for the phone company.

Usually Audrey hated surprises. Mainly because she'd had so many of them in her life, and few—if any—had been enjoyable. But suddenly, much to her astonishment, she discovered that surprises could actually be quite pleasant. As long as Wheeler Rush was involved.

"I, uh...I haven't had dinner yet," he said suddenly. "In fact, I was kind of headed in that direction myself. Would you—"

He hesitated a moment, and Audrey's heart sank a little. He didn't really want to ask her out, she told herself. He was just being polite. And even at that, he was having to decide just how polite he thought he should be.

"Would you like to grab a bite with me?" he finally asked, his smile *almost* convincing. "I was just going to try this new place a couple of blocks up Bardstown Road. It's inexpensive, but the food is supposed to be very good. We could walk there."

"In the rain?" she asked. Then, before she could stop herself, she added, "Isn't once enough for you?"

Invariably, her thoughts had returned to the day they had been caught in the downpour, the day Mr. Rush had loaned her his spare change of clothes—which she hadn't yet returned, because she'd been hoping he would forget about them, and then she'd be able to keep them forever and ever, and take them out on days when she wasn't working for him anymore, and hold them to her nose and sniff them to remind herself of him, though she had no idea why she would want to do such a thing. Then the thought of rain reminded her of the couple she had viewed across the street earlier—the ones sharing a kiss beneath an umbrella—and that made her feel sadder still.

"The rain's stopping," he said, smiling, obviously oblivious to the train of her troubled thoughts. "It's barely a drizzle out there now. Besides..."

"What?" she said when he offered no indication that he would finish the statement.

He shrugged lightly. "I kind of like walking in the rain with you, Miss Finnegan."

Oh, she thought. Oh, that was just so sweet.

And then she realized how weird things had suddenly become. This was like one of her romantic boss fantasies coming way too close to life—the one where he surprised her at home and asked her out on the spur of the moment, and they wound up necking on the sofa. It was her second-favorite boss fantasy, right after the one where they accidentally ran into each other at the travel agency, and he asked her to take a trip with him to the Bahamas on the spur of the moment, and they ended up necking in the surf.

Audrey shook both fantasies off before they could take hold. Something was definitely going on here that made absolutely no sense. Had she fallen asleep in her pot pie? she wondered. Was this the onset of some strange, fast-acting, delusion-causing food poisoning?

Then again, did it really matter?

"Okay," she agreed readily. "Thanks. If you don't mind, I'd love to join you. But we'll go Dutch, right?"

He opened his mouth again, and she knew he was going to object, so she stood her ground.

"I won't go unless you let me pay my way," she insisted. There. That ought to put an end to those silly fantasies. She *never* paid her own way in her daydreams.

"All right, fine," he conceded with obvious reluctance. "You can pay for your own dinner. This time."

Well, that certainly sounded promising. Audrey had to force down the bubbles of delight that effervesced in her midsection. "O-okay," she said. "Just let me clean up in here and go change my clothes. I'll only take a minute."

Wheeler was still trying to figure out what had possessed him to ask his secretary—his *temporary* secretary—to join him for dinner when she exited the bathroom some moments later. She'd shed her sweats and T-shirt in favor of black leggings and a black tunic...and black shoes and black jewelry, he noted further with a mental shake of his head. But she hadn't bothered with cosmetics, and her hair

tumbled free past her shoulders in a riot of blue-black curls.
He'd had no idea her hair was that long, and suddenly, for
some bizarre reason, all he wanted to do was reach out and
tangle his fingers in the silky mass, to see if it felt as soft
as it looked.

When she'd opened her front door to him, he hadn't been
able to believe she was the same person who came to work
for him every morning. The Miss Finnegan he knew was
always perfectly coiffed and manicured and made up, and
dressed in something snug and bright. At home, however,
she obviously preferred not to go to all that trouble. Or
brightness.

And strangely, even though he had, of course, taken note
of her snug, bright, revealing, suggestive, absolutely-
nothing-left-to-the-imagination, uh... Where was he? Oh,
yeah. Even though he had taken note of her attire—over
and over again—it was this side of her that roused the
strongest feelings in him. Feelings, he marveled further,
that were almost akin to...affection.

She seemed more approachable now, more human, more
womanly, if such a thing were possible. Not a secretary.
Not a temp. Not a tight skirt and sweater. Not even a walking, talking fountain of bad luck. But a woman. Miss Finnegan, he realized for the first time, was more than a pretty
face and a curvy body and a font of misfortune. She had a
home. She had cats. She had T-shirts with funny sayings
on them. She had chicken pot pie.

And all those things, when taken in combination with the
woman who showed up at his office every day, added up
to one very intriguing individual. One Wheeler simply
couldn't help but find attractive.

Not a good reaction to have, he told himself. There were
so many reasons why he shouldn't get involved with Miss
Finnegan that he could be up all night listing them. For one
thing, she was working for him, and he'd witnessed for
himself at his old job that office romances, particularly

those between boss and secretary, simply weren't a good idea at all. In addition to that, she was only working for him temporarily—and there was just no telling how that was going to go.

Still, it did explain why he'd suddenly asked her out. Because she was really cute. And she made him smile. And she roused some very warm, wistful, wonderful feelings inside him—deep inside him, in a place he'd never explored before.

Oh, yeah. And also because he hadn't quite been able to rid his mind of the image of her standing on his desk, changing a lightbulb, earlier in the week. He'd returned from lunch to find her work station empty, and had assumed she'd left for a bite to eat. So he'd simply continued blithely on into his own office as casually as you please, never suspecting he would be flummoxed by what he saw once he arrived there.

Flummoxed. Truly. Of all things.

But there she'd been, standing on tiptoe on his desk, her yellow high heels neglected on the floor. She'd been reaching up—way, waaaay up—to twist a halogen bulb into one of the recessed holes in the ceiling. As a result, her bright yellow miniskirt had been riding *very* high on her yellow stocking-clad thighs, and her little yellow sweater had hiked up over the waistband to reveal what appeared to be a race car Band-Aid marring that tantalizing bit of flesh that had driven Wheeler to distraction since her first day at work.

As if pulled by an invisible thread, he'd moved slowly, silently, toward his desk, halting only when he realized that one step further would have put him in the position of looking up her skirt. So he'd squeezed his eyes shut—tight—and had asked what on earth she thought she was doing up there.

Falling, that's what, he'd realized belatedly. Startled by his sudden presence, she had jolted like a live wire. Although she'd dropped the lightbulb, in an amazing—and unusual—reaction of swift grace, she had managed to catch it again. Unfortunately, though, she had stepped on his lucky mechanical pencil in the process and snapped that sucker right in two. That, in turn, had caused her to yelp in pain—presumably because she'd jabbed her foot with the lead—and had sent her tumbling off the desk and right into Wheeler's arms.

And all he'd been able to think about in that moment was how soft and lush and strangely right her body felt pressed against his own, and about how very much he wanted to kiss her.

But since that would have been disastrous, not to mention a violation of professional etiquette, he had satisfied himself with simply gazing into her eyes—her huge, clear, pale green eyes, those eyes that put the depths of the greenest sea to shame—as he eased her down to the floor in front of him. And he'd tried to ignore the rapid-fire thumping of his heart as he did so. But that maneuver had failed miserably, because Miss Finnegan hadn't immediately moved away from him, had instead gazed right back into his eyes and had parted her lips as if she, too, were suffering from the same afflictions as Wheeler was at that moment.

And now he told himself that asking her out was just going to cause more trouble, because it wasn't likely to assuage whatever strange longing he'd suddenly developed for her. In fact, the more he thought about it now, the more he realized what a colossal mistake he was making in encouraging anything of a personal nature to develop between them. More than anything else right now, Wheeler needed for something—anything—to go *right*. Audrey Finnegan, he knew, was not that anything. She was instead the most clumsy, unfortunate woman he had ever met.

He was in no position at this point in his life to be starting a relationship with anyone. He was virtually broke, was struggling to save a business…his entire life was simply in a state of upheaval. He had neither the time nor the emotional energy to expend on nurturing a budding romance. Certainly Miss Finnegan was a nice, attractive woman, one who, under other circumstances—much better, much more fortunate circumstances—he might want to get to know more intimately. But this just wasn't a good time for him. There were too many other things that required his attention.

Good-luck charm or no, anything personal he might pursue with the woman was bound to be doomed, just as everything else in his life lately had been. She was one of those people who were best kept at arm's length, if not farther. There was just no telling what would go wrong when Audrey Finnegan was around.

And for a man like Wheeler, who had fallen into a major slump out of which he still hadn't quite worked his way, to embroil himself any deeper with a woman like Miss Finnegan... Well, it might very well prove to be a fatal combination. Fatal to his professional life—and perhaps his sanity—at any rate.

In spite of all of his assurances, however, he couldn't quite quell the warmth that wound through him as he watched her approach him. Because somehow, in spite of the bad luck that seemed to walk hand in hand with her, she instilled in Wheeler an odd sense of well-being. And somehow he just couldn't quite shake the feeling that he was so very lucky to have had her walk into his life the way she had.

"All set?" he asked.

She nodded, her eyes seeming even brighter than usual. "Ready when you are."

The rain had ended by the time they left her apartment, leaving in its wake an evening that was cool and fresh, redolent of springtime about to burst into full bloom. For some reason, as they strode along, Wheeler began to feel nervous, as if he were back in junior high school, walking

Marianne Monroe home from school for the first time. Something about Miss Finnegan made him feel like an adolescent again. And not just because of the hormonal surges, either. So, true to eighth-grade mentality, all Wheeler could do was make small talk as they made their way down the street.

"So...you mentioned that you moved here not long ago?" he began. "Brought the big snows with you that winter?" he added with a smile.

She nodded, but didn't smile back, evidently not realizing that he was joking. "I grew up in California, but my mom is from here, so I have a lot of cousins in the area. I visited here a lot when I was a kid, and it seemed like a nice place to live. Plus, I really needed to move away from the West Coast. So this was the logical choice."

"What made you leave California?"

"Earthquakes," she replied succinctly.

"You're afraid of earthquakes?" he asked, fully understanding how one might be put off by something like plate tectonics, particularly when the tectonics of those plates were happening right under one's feet.

She glanced up at him, her expression confused. "No, I'm not afraid of them at all. I meant I had to leave because I think I was causing most of them. The earthquake activity in my part of California has slowed down quite a bit since I left."

Wheeler opened his mouth to reply, then realized he had absolutely no idea what to say, so closed it again.

"Of course, the tornado activity here has increased in direct correlation to my arrival," she added. "And there was that big spring flood not too long ago. So I might have to try another part of the country before long."

Wheeler narrowed his eyes in bemusement, knowing only that he had to dissuade her of that idea. Not just the one about her causing tornadoes and high water, but the one about her relocating to another part of the country, too.

Simply put, he didn't want to see her going far away. He wasn't sure why—he just didn't.

"Miss Finnegan," he began in as comforting a voice as he could rouse, "I assure you as a Louisville native that life on a river like the Ohio tends to bring with it the occasional flood. And tornadoes are something we just have to live with. It's always been that way. Every spring brings its threat of foul weather. You have nothing to do with either of those natural phenomena. Trust me. It's geographic. Honest."

She didn't look convinced of his assurances when she said, "Well, if it makes you feel better to believe that, fine. *I'm* certainly not going to say anything to change your mind about it."

He narrowed his eyes again, this time in utter befuddlement. Never had he met anyone like Audrey Finnegan. "Well," he said, injecting his voice with a cheerfulness that was in no way feigned, "California's loss is our gain, I'm sure."

She smiled shyly, something that made the strings of his heart go *zing*. "Thanks," she murmured. "It's nice of you to say that."

They strode in silence for some moments, then Miss Finnegan jump-started the conversation again when she said, "Did you know that Mr. Skolnik at Davenport's is going to go into business for himself before the year is out?"

That surprised Wheeler. Not just that old man Skolnik would start an entrepreneurial venture just shy of his retirement date, but also that Miss Finnegan would know about it. Or would know Mr. Skolnik, for that matter. "How did you hear about that?"

"Mr. Skolnik told me."

"You know Rupert Skolnik?" he asked. Amazing. For someone who had only lived in town for a handful of years, Miss Finnegan seemed to have an endless supply of acquaintances—and from all walks of life, too.

She nodded. "I had to call Davenport's to update their file at the office, and he and I got to talking. He's a very nice man. I told him you'd be glad to help him out when he gets started. You ask me, I think he'd be a great client. Very dependable."

Wheeler expelled a little chuckle. "Well, thank you, Miss Finnegan, for keeping me in mind when it came time for recommendations."

She smiled at him. "Don't mention it."

For the rest of the evening, conversation flowed smoothly, if none too deeply. Over dinner—where, surprisingly, no food or beverage left the table—Miss Finnegan told Wheeler all about the Finnegan curse that had plagued her family for generations. Not that he bought a word of it, naturally, in spite of her propensity for misfortune. Then he, in turn, shared with her snippets of his own past. The Rushes, on the other hand, he told her, had always been blessed with nothing but *good* fortune.

In fact, he added at one point, when he was in college studying Shakespeare, he had come to the conclusion that he must be descended from one of the sets of lovers from *A Midsummer Night's Dream,* who were blessed by the fairies at the end of the play. That was the only way he could explain the long line of good luck and happiness that the Rushes had enjoyed. Magic must be at the root of it, so prevalent were the good times and good fortune in his family. There could be no other explanation for it.

"You're a romantic," Miss Finnegan told him as they strode home some time later. "Only a romantic could come up with that fairy theory."

The sky had turned dark by now, and dozens of scattered stars played hide-and-seek with the running wisps of clouds overhead. The promise of rain still hung heavy in the air, and the breeze was a damp kiss on Wheeler's cheek. He hastened his step a bit, fearing another storm was close at hand. But all the while he hated to hurry the end to his time with his temporary secretary. Especially since he knew there was a whole day to get through between now and the next time he saw her.

"A romantic?" he echoed as he went, chuckling at the very idea of such a thing. "Hardly. I'm far too pragmatic to be romantic. Romance is…"

"What?" she asked, matching his stride effortlessly with those long, long legs of hers, as if she, too, sensed the coming rain and wanted to avoid another drenching.

He shrugged. "I don't know. I guess I've just never really experienced romance, that's all. Therefore, pragmatic as I am, it can't possibly exist."

She laughed at that, a rich, joyful sound that warmed him to the depths of his soul. "Romance exists," she assured him. "You just have to know where to look for it. It takes different forms for different people. Sometimes it sneaks up on you, and sometimes you have to go on an all-out safari to find it."

She met his gaze levelly, as if she were studying him, trying to figure him out. Then, in a quiet, thoughtful voice, she added, "But you can't tell me that anyone who comes from a family as lucky as yours has never experienced romance. Romance and good luck go hand in hand. That's a fact of life."

He hedged, not sure how to answer. "Well…*I* haven't experienced it," he told her.

She eyed him with much consideration for a moment longer. "You've never been married?" she asked.

He shook his head. "No. Not even close."

"Never been in love?"

"Not really."

"Never wanted to be in love?"

"Well, I wouldn't say *that*," he replied.

Though what, exactly, had made him reply in such a way, he couldn't possibly have said. *Did* he want to be in love? He'd never really thought about it. Love seemed like one of those things that just sort of happened to a person, whether you wanted it to or not, whether you were expecting it or not. And *wanting* to be in love simply seemed like a foregone conclusion. Love made the world go around, according to all the poets. Who didn't want to be in love?

Then again, who did?

She smiled, and something about the gesture sent a wave of heated bliss shooting right through Wheeler's midsection. Wow, she was pretty. Even in the dark, she seemed illuminated somehow. Like a maiden in one of those paintings where the artist used gilt to illustrate the purity of his subject. She was just that striking.

"So then you *do* want to be in love," she said, turning the assumption into a statement instead of a question.

He chuckled again, but suddenly felt very confused. "Well, I wouldn't say that, either," he replied softly, at a loss as to how to answer her.

Just how had they gotten started on this conversation? Wheeler wondered wildly. One minute, they'd been discussing earthquakes and tornadoes, and the next minute, they'd lit on matters of the heart. Leave it to Miss Finnegan to take a perfectly bland discussion about natural phenomena and turn it into something meaningful. Then again, when he got right down to it, he could argue that earthquakes and tornadoes had quite a bit in common with matters of the heart, didn't they?

She made a quiet *tsking* sound under her breath and shook her head slowly. "Boy, just like a man," she said softly.

Her observation brought him back to the matter at hand. "What's just like a man? What are you talking about?"

She waved a hand airily in front of her. "Oh, you guys can't make up your minds about anything."

He gaped at her. "I beg your pardon. I thought it was

women who couldn't make up their minds about anything."

She shook her head, her ebony curls dancing about her shoulders when she did. And again Wheeler found himself wanting to reach out and twist one of the silky loops around each finger.

"No, that's just a popular myth," she said. "One of those...what do you call them? Urban legends."

He smiled. "I thought urban legends were those stories about the sheep man and the vanishing hitchhiker and things like that. I'm afraid I don't follow you on this one."

She arched her eyebrows philosophically. "Well, no offense, Mr. Rush, but that doesn't surprise me at all."

He was about to press the issue when he realized she had stopped walking, and he noted—with surprising disappointment—that they were standing in front of her apartment house. The big brick Victorian rose dark against the sky, lamplight glowing yellow in some of the apartments on the lower floors. As he gazed at the looming structure, Wheeler felt a splatter of water fall on his nose. That was followed by another. And then another. And another, and another.

"Oh, no," Miss Finnegan gasped beside him, hurrying up the concrete stairs toward the covered porch. "Here comes the rain. Quick—come inside."

Instead of questioning the wisdom of that particular edict, Wheeler immediately obeyed, racing up the steps behind her, laughing when they reached the porch overhang just as the skies opened up and began to lash the earth with fat, furious raindrops. A rumble of thunder overhead told them that the downpour would probably continue for some time, and he breathed a sigh of... What? he wondered. Relief? That it was raining again? Why would that make him feel relieved? Now he would have to stay here with—

Oh.

"That was lucky," he said aloud when he realized his

time with Miss Finnegan would be necessarily extended until the rain stopped. In spite of his happiness with such a development, it was something that only compounded his confusion.

"You mean *un*lucky," she corrected him.

"No," he said, suddenly realizing just how fortuitous the situation was. "We made it just in time. We almost got drenched."

"But now you're stranded here," she pointed out unnecessarily. "You can't walk home in that." As if to punctuate her statement, a flash of lightning split the sky, followed immediately by a rousing *BOOM* of thunder.

And being stranded here with her was unlucky? he repeated to himself. Obviously Miss Finnegan really didn't know good fortune when it was right beneath her nose.

"I don't mind," he said, surprised to realize that was the truth. He'd had an astonishingly good time tonight, and he was reluctant to see it end just yet. "If you can stand me hanging around for a little while, I mean. If it doesn't let up soon, I'll just walk home in the rain. I'd at least like to wait until the lightning stops, though."

He told himself the only reason she looked anxious when he voiced his intentions was because they were standing in semidarkness, and her features were shadowed by the spastic beam of the yellow bug light behind them. Why on earth would his presence make her uncomfortable after the evening they'd just spent together? What else could her seeming anxiety be but a trick of the light?

"I…I guess I don't mind," she said. Then she hastened to add, "I mean…of course I don't mind. It's not safe walking in a storm like this one. Come on in," she added as she reached for the front door. "I'll fix us some coffee."

Five

"Truly, Miss Finnegan, coffee isn't necessary."

"Are you sure?"

"Oh, absolutely. I've never been more sure of anything in my entire life."

Audrey inhaled a deep, steadying breath as she closed the door behind them, but another rousing thump of thunder had her jumping nearly a foot off the ground. Still, she knew it wasn't the surly storm outside that had her feeling so tense and jittery. It was the presence of her boss, right here in her home, looking yummy enough to eat.

Her stomach flip-flopped about a million times as she hurried past Mr. Rush and entered the living area, switching on a floor lamp to afford them some small measure of light. Her employer followed behind her, his boot heels scuffing lightly over the hardwood floors, the sound resonating through her entire system. When she spun around to look at him, he seemed somehow larger than usual in the close confines of the tiny apartment. He seemed more casual. More intimate. And he looked...

Oh, my.

She had been on edge all night long, ever since she'd opened her front door to find him standing there. The way he had looked at her then... The way he continued to look at her now... Honestly. She nearly burst into flames every time her eyes met his. There was something different about him tonight, and not just his sexy, dressed-down duds, either. He'd been more relaxed, more approachable, more human tonight. And Audrey had responded to that humanness way too quickly, way too needfully, way too irreversibly.

And the longer the two of them were together like this, the closer they came to fulfilling that boss fantasy of hers that she hadn't been able to shake all evening—which, she had to admit, she had mixed feelings about. This was just too weird, the way everything was falling in place, and she couldn't help feeling that she was somehow skirting the edge of reality. All they needed now was for the power to go out, and then to realize in a rush of recognition how much they had come to love and need each other over the past two weeks, and then they could fall onto the sofa, fulfill every decadent dream she'd ever had, then ride off into the sunset and live happily ever after, fade to black.

Audrey turned her attention to the lamp she had just switched on. *Anytime now,* she thought. Unfortunately—or perhaps fortunately, she amended, thinking it strange that she might for once in her life be lucky, at the one time when she really didn't want to be—the bulb didn't so much as flicker.

Just as well, she thought. She was totally unprepared for sharing anything more personal than coffee with her employer. And he'd said he didn't even want that from her.

"You should have called me to help you move," he said, startling her back to the moment. Boy, she was jumpy tonight. He gestured toward the boxes scattered about. "I would have been happy to lend a hand."

"Oh, thanks, but that's okay," she replied, marveling at how breathy and rushed her voice suddenly sounded. Kathleen Turner had nothing on her. "There wasn't that much. I had a couple of my cousins come over and lift the big stuff."

He nodded, but said nothing more. Things became awkward again, and Audrey found herself praying for an end to the rain as soon as possible. At this rate, with the way her stomach was rolling around, her boss was going to see a side of her she'd just as soon not show him—namely, her backside as she heaved over the toilet.

But instead of abating, the thunder and lightning outside only grew more furious. The wind battered the house, pelting the windows with rain, shaking the trees beyond. If this kept up, she thought, it would be hours before the storm ended.

"Uh," she began, striving to say something—anything—that would alleviate the tension winding through her. "Too bad I don't have the cable hooked up yet. We could check the Weather Channel to see how bad it's going to get."

She neglected to add that it would be some time before the cable was hooked up—if ever. Not unless she could hold on to her latest job as a temp for longer than she had kept her last dozen jobs. And call her overly cautious, but pouncing on her employer, wrestling him to the ground and having her way with him was probably a pretty good way to lose it. She'd be wise to remember that.

But her boss didn't look too concerned. "I wouldn't worry about it," he said as he sauntered slowly, easily—sexily—into the room. "I'm sure the storm will blow over soon enough."

The closer he drew to her, the more Audrey's heart leaped and danced. She could almost feel his heat, his life, as he approached her. When she inhaled a deep breath to steady her erratic heart rate, her nose and lungs filled with the scent of him. And that only made her heart race that much faster.

"Uh," she tried again, "you know...now that I think about it, you could help me out here." She fled to the flowered chintz sofa that her beefy cousins had scooted against the wall earlier that afternoon. "I just decided this evening that I don't like my couch where it is. I think it would look better over there under the windows, don't you?"

He seemed to give the matter weighty consideration for a moment, then nodded. "Yeah, you know, I think it would."

"I bet if we both put our backs into it, we could get it over there with no trouble."

He waved a hand at her negligently. "Please. Miss Finnegan. I think I can move a couch by myself."

"But it's pretty heavy."

The look he gave her told her he thought she was being silly. "Allow me," he said.

He moved toward the piece of furniture in question and stooped beside it, gripping it resolutely underneath with both hands. With one hefty groan, he pushed himself up, lifting that end, then began to pull the couch toward the part of the room she had indicated. Everything was moving along nicely—he had just about cleared the windows—when, out of nowhere, Roxanne and Marco appeared, evidently having decided this would be a good time for Championship Feline Wrestling.

To say their timing was off would have been like saying Martha Stewart was pretty good at throwing parties. But then, they were cats, weren't they? Never thinking about anyone but themselves. They bolted across the living room at the speed of light, aiming, naturally, straight for Mr. Rush's feet. Around and around they lapped him, until they were absolutely certain that he had lost his footing. Then, with all the finesse of a hockey goalie, the two cats disappeared.

Leaving Mr. Rush to take a spectacular fall.

He landed on his fanny with the couch across his shins, which, to Audrey's way of thinking, looked really, really painful. Her suspicions were pretty much confirmed by the blood-curdling cry her boss emitted as the sofa came crashing down on his legs. Without hesitation she hurried to free him, lifting the couch high enough for him to pull himself clear. Immediately he doubled up his entire body, pulling his legs up before him, hugging his shins to his chest.

"Oh, Mr. Rush," Audrey said as she set the couch back down and crouched beside him. "I'm sorry. I am so, so sorry. I can't believe Roxanne and Marco were so rude. Are you okay? Is anything broken? Can you stand?"

Should I just go ahead and give you my resignation now? Or would you rather fire me yourself in the morning?

He gritted his teeth and blew air in and out of his mouth at an alarming rate. Then, very, very carefully, he muttered, "Yes, I think I'm okay. No, I don't think anything is broken. And yes, I think, if I tried hard enough, I could stand. But if it's all the same to you, I believe I'd rather just sit here and suffer for a moment. That was quite... unpleasant."

"I'm sorry," she said again. She nibbled her lip fretfully. "How about a couple of ice packs?" she asked.

He nodded roughly. "I think that would probably be an enormous help. Thank you."

As grateful to have something to do with her hands besides reach for him as she was to be doing something helpful, she raced to the kitchen and loaded up two sandwich bags with ice. Then, after wrapping a dish towel around each, she returned to the living room. Mr. Rush had moved to sit on the sofa that had wounded him, and was bent over, gingerly rubbing his shins.

"Thank you," he said again as he reached for the ice packs. He held one on each limb, pressing them gently over his blue jeans, and avoided looking at Audrey.

"You're welcome," she replied automatically. Then, because she wasn't sure she had said it often enough, she added, "I'm sorry. I'm really, really sorry."

He glanced up at her. "It wasn't your fault, Miss Finnegan."

Somehow she knew he didn't believe that any more than she did. She sat down beside him on the sofa, making sure to keep at least a good, solid foot of space between them, and told him, "I'll send Roxanne and Marco to bed tonight without any kibble. I can't believe they did that."

He sighed heavily before assuring her, "It's all right. Don't send them to bed kibbleless. I'm sure it was an accident. They couldn't possibly have done it on purpose."

She eyed him thoughtfully. "You've never owned cats, have you, Mr. Rush?"

"No, why?"

She shook her head. "I could just tell, that's all."

"Well," he began again. "Just…promise me you like the sofa *exactly* where it is."

She managed a halfhearted smile. "It looks great. Really. I wouldn't move it another inch. Thank you. It was very sweet of you to help me out at risk of life and limb. Or rather, limbs. Plural."

And then, although she had no idea what possessed her to do it—well, maybe she had *some* idea what possessed her…just not one she wanted to consider too deeply—she leaned forward and kissed him softly, chastely on the cheek.

As soon as she completed the quick caress, however, she realized she shouldn't have done it. And not just because it was a professional faux pas, but because performing such a simple, yet intimate, gesture just made her want more— more of something she knew she would never have.

She started to pull back, blushing in the process, because she couldn't *believe* she had acted on such an unwarranted impulse. But she never quite managed to move away completely. Not because she stopped herself. Because Mr. Rush did.

Before she realized what he intended to do, he had dropped one of the ice packs and reached behind her to curl his fingers over the hair at her nape, an action that effectively halted her backward progress. Startled, she looked at his face, only to find that his eyes were fairly ablaze with a yearning kind of fire that she told herself must simply be a reflection of what was burning inside her.

For one long moment, neither of them moved. They only gazed into each other's eyes, as if neither could quite believe what was happening. Then the fingers at Audrey's nape skimmed up and down once, twice, three times, before curling tighter and winding in her hair. And then, slowly, slowly, oh...so slowly, he gently pulled her forward again.

There was no way she could have stopped the kiss, even if she'd wanted to. Which, of course, she didn't. He brushed his lips gently over hers, opening his mouth slightly as he did so, the motion so swift, so soft, so seductive, she almost wondered if she had imagined it. He followed up that initial caress with another just like it. Then, evidently gaining more confidence, he covered her mouth completely with his.

A dozen tiny explosions detonated in Audrey's belly, rocketing to every nerve she possessed. All she could do was sit there, leaning forward, not daring to touch him anywhere other than where he was holding her. She feared if she did, he would come to his senses and stop kissing her. So she followed his lead as best she could, tilting her head first left, and then right, to facilitate what was fast becoming a very interesting exploration.

For long moments he only grazed her mouth with his, pushing his fingers deeply into the hair above her nape, urging her closer...closer...closer. Bit by bit, inch by inch, Audrey let him draw her nearer, until she couldn't tolerate even the scant few inches left between them. Unable to keep from touching him any longer, she lifted one hand to his shoulder, the other to his hair, and let herself be swept away completely by the kiss.

He responded to her silent encouragement by immediately dropping the other ice pack to the floor and roping his arm around her waist, crushing her body to his. And in no time at all, what had begun as a subtle exploration turned into a full-bodied assault on her senses. What could she do but surrender to him? Especially since that was exactly what she wanted to do.

So Audrey succumbed to the desires and needs and appetites that had plagued her since that first day at work, when she'd noted her boss was one tall, dark and very handsome customer. She tunneled her fingers through the silk of his hair, cupped his rough jaw in her hand and kissed him back for all she was worth.

In response he uttered a quiet, desperate sound and began to fall back onto the sofa, taking Audrey down along with him. He tangled one hand in the mass of curls that spilled down her back, as if he just couldn't quite bring himself to release them. The other hand he opened at the small of her back, his fingers splaying across her waist, urging her lower, lower, lower, along with him. She willingly allowed him to lead her down, until she lay fully atop him, her breasts crushed against his chest, her belly pressed to his, her legs interwoven with his.

And then her boss really got down to business.

The hand at her waist instantly crept lower, until he had curved his fingers over the elegant curve of her derriere. Audrey gasped at the contact, and he took advantage of her reaction to taste her more deeply, filling her mouth with his tongue, raiding, pillaging, consuming. In response she urged the hand at his jaw lower, skimming her fingers down

the strong column of his throat, along the line of his broad
shoulder, over the plump biceps that strained beneath her
fingertips. Her fingers tripped lightly down each rib until
she located the hem of his sweater. And then, unable to
stop herself, Audrey went on a little exploration of her own.

Beneath his sweater she encountered heated, satin steel.
His flesh came alive everywhere she touched him, his muscles bunching and dancing under her palm. He groaned as
she scooted her hand upward, the sound emerging as something feral and unrestrained. As she tangled her fingers in
the silky hair scattered across his chest and lower, he
pressed his hand more intimately, more insistently, against
her fanny, pushing her into the cradle of his thighs. Instinctively she rubbed against him, feeling him ripen and bloom
against her. As if he'd thoroughly lost control of things, he
bucked up against her, a vague promise of what would
come later.

"Oh," Audrey murmured in utter delight. "Oh, Mr.
Rush…"

The sound of his name, so formal in such an intimate
joining of their bodies, stopped him cold. Immediately he
halted the sweet assault on her senses, retreating with a jerk
that banged the back of his head on the armrest of the sofa.
He didn't even seem to register the contact, however, as he
was too busy gazing into Audrey's eyes with what she
could only liken to pure, unadulterated terror.

Her heart sank at the realization, shattering into a million
billion pieces. She couldn't imagine what had made him
kiss her that first time, but whatever it was, he had now
reconsidered it in a big, big way. And he had clearly come
to the conclusion that he'd made a major mistake.

"Miss Finnegan, I—"

But he didn't finish whatever it was he'd intended to say.
Instead he only continued to stare at her in complete silence. Or, more accurately, he continued to stare at her
mouth. For a moment she thought maybe she'd been mis-

taken about his reaction, and that he was going to kiss her again. Then, in an awkward but gentle jumble of limbs, he pushed her up and off him, settling her at one end of the sofa. Then he folded himself into a seated position at the other end, burying his face in his hands.

Audrey didn't know what to do. One minute she'd been living out her wildest dreams and the next she was feeling as if she should apologize for something that she hadn't even started. So she scooted back as far into the corner of the sofa as she could, wishing there was some way to take back the last few minutes and lock them away in a dark and secret place deep inside where only she would remember them.

"So," she said lamely, "I guess this means you're feeling better?"

She wasn't sure, but she thought he expelled a sound of dubious humor at that. He nodded slowly, almost imperceptibly. "Yes, thank you. My legs, at least, are feeling much better."

Audrey, too, nodded. "Well…that's something."

He inhaled a deep breath and expelled it slowly. "Oh, it certainly was that. Something, I mean."

"Mr. Rush, I—"

He glanced up, and the look of abject misery on his face completely cut off her words. Thankfully he didn't look directly at Audrey, but focused his gaze on the wall opposite. "I think," he said softly, "considering all we've been through tonight, you could call me Wheeler."

She grinned, feeling a little more hopeful. At least he hadn't fired her. "Then you absolutely have to call me Audrey," she told him. "It's been driving me crazy, you calling me Miss Finnegan all the time. It makes me feel like an heiress or a first-grade teacher or something, which I most assuredly am *not*."

He chuckled, and finally turned to look at her. "All right, Audrey," he said.

For some reason she got the feeling that he liked calling her that. Maybe it was the little twinkle in his eyes that became more luminous when he said her name. Or maybe it was the warm smile that played about his lips. Or maybe it was the soft purr that colored his voice when he enunciated *Audrey* as if it were a lullaby.

"Then I guess it's settled," he added. Suddenly he tensed, all vestiges of that brief warmth evaporating in one swift instant. "The name thing, at least, is settled. As for the other thing…"

His voice trailed off, but there was no mistaking what other thing he was talking about. There was just something about getting horizontal with a guy that sort of went beyond simple conversation. And when the guy you got horizontal with was Wheeler Rush, not to mention the guy who signed your paychecks, well…forget about it.

"Mr. Rush, I—"

"Wheeler," he quickly interjected.

She swallowed hard before saying, "Wheeler." Still, she did like the way his name felt and sounded coming out of her mouth like that. "What just happened here tonight… I mean…that is… What I'm trying to say—"

She sighed heavily, scrubbed her hands restlessly through her hair and gave it one more shot. "Sometimes," she said softly, tentatively, hopefully, "these things just happen, and if you try to figure out why, it'll make your brain explode." She offered him a halfhearted smile, hoping it looked more convincing than it felt. "So let's just chalk it up to the storm outside and a nice dinner and leave it at that. In fact, if you want, we can just forget it ever happened and never mention it again."

He eyed her doubtfully. "You think you can forget that ever happened?"

She nodded quickly. Too quickly. There could be no doubt for either of them that she was lying through her teeth. "Sure. Sure, I can forget it. Can't you?"

He hesitated for a moment, then he nodded, too, in exactly the same way. "Yeah," he said, obviously lying as bald-facedly as she was. "I can forget it, too. We'll just, um…just, uh…" He inhaled deeply and released the breath in a slow, ragged stream. "We'll just pretend it never happened," he finished in a tone of voice that was in no way certain.

"Okay, then," she said softly. "No problem."

"We, uh…we just won't mention it again," he said, echoing her earlier words. He glanced out the window then, and hurried on, "Looks like the rain might be letting up." A rousing burst of thunder underscored the fact that he was still lying shamelessly. "I should probably try to make a run for it."

She nodded, following him up when he stood. He tested one leg, then the other, taking a few experimental steps before scooping up the ice packs and heading for the kitchen. He dropped them in the sink, then crossed the tiny room to the front door.

"I think I'll live," he said when he successfully covered the distance without collapsing.

She forced a smile. "That's good to hear. After all, my first payday comes up next week."

He laughed lightly, but it sounded unnatural somehow. "Well. I'll just see you Monday morning then, right?"

"Right."

An awkward moment ensued, and Audrey scrambled for something to say that would alleviate the heaviness that seemed to fill the air. But no words came to her rescue, so she only stood silently, stupidly, staring at her boss and wishing like crazy that things had turned out differently. Wishing that she understood even half of what had just passed between them. Wishing she knew what it was that bound them still.

He twisted the knob and jerked the door open, throwing another one of those awkward smiles over his shoulder as he passed through it. "Good night, Audrey," he said as he left.

"'Night," she replied. "And thanks…Wheeler. For everything."

Only after he had disappeared down the stairs did she close the door behind him and reluctantly twist the bolt. For a long time she only leaned back against the door and replayed the evening's events in her head, wondering when exactly things had changed between her and her employer. And she wondered, too, what had made him pull back the way he had, just when things were getting interesting.

She'd been fully willing to continue on their sensual journey herself, to see where it might lead. But even though he had started it, something had made him change his mind. And she, coward that she was, hadn't quite been willing to delve into why. Maybe, she thought, because she really didn't want to know why.

Audrey wasn't entirely clueless about life and love—she knew, for example, that men were totally unfathomable when it came to romance and intimacy. She didn't have a lot of experience with…with…with *that,* but she had enough to know that she would never understand what men wanted, or why they behaved the way they did. Even though she couldn't figure them out, she still managed to work around all their little male idiosyncrasies to create some kind of tolerable situation with them. With Wheeler, however…

Well, suffice it to say that he was…what was that word? An enigma. Yeah, that was it.

She was still pondering that particular dilemma when her gaze lit on the housewarming gift he'd brought her and which she hadn't yet opened. The small, square, gaily wrapped package—obviously completed by a department store or boutique, because no man would ever take the pains necessary to make a present look that pretty—sat benignly on her kitchen table, as if asking, *Well? What are you waiting for? An engraved invitation?*

"No," Audrey said aloud. "I'm not waiting for anything."

True to her word, she made her way to the table, hesitating for only a moment before tearing into the package like a four-year-old at Christmastime. Inside she found something wrapped in white tissue paper. Lifting it gingerly, she carefully rearranged the folds until she located the prize within. And when she did, she smiled, a flutter of delight tickling her tummy and caressing her to the ends of her toes.

What Wheeler had given her for a housewarming present was a ceramic horseshoe to hang on the wall. It was a little bigger than hand size, painted white and decorated with an arcing row of delicate four-leaf clovers. A card was nestled amid the tissue, and she hastily withdrew it from the envelope and unfolded it, too, to read the sentiment he'd inscribed.

For all the luck you've brought me, may this return a bit to you. Be sure to hang it over your front door with the U facing up, so you don't lose the luck. At least, that's what my mother always taught me. Thank you for so many things. And welcome to the neighborhood.

Sincerely, Wheeler Rush.

As Audrey stood in her kitchen cradling her gift, the way she would the crown jewels of England, all she could think was that, when it came to bosses, she was the luckiest secretary alive.

It was just too bad, she thought further, that he was only temporary.

Six

Fortunately for Wheeler, in the two months that followed his dubious romantic interlude with Audrey Finnegan, he scarcely had a chance to reflect upon it. Which was just as well, because reflecting upon it only led to daydreams and fantasies that no employer should ever be having about the woman who worked for him. Not unless he wanted to find himself standing before a senate subcommittee defending his choice of video rental selections.

He still had no idea what had caused him to react to her the way he had that night at her apartment. She had simply been too close, too warm, too pretty, too sweet smelling, too intoxicating. He hadn't been able to help himself when he'd reached for her.

On those few occasions when he *did* find himself thinking about what had happened that night—trying to figure out just what the hell it had all meant—he grew hot and muddled and confused, something that was in no way conducive to good work habits. And he had really needed to have good work habits for those two months following that ill-fated tryst with his temporary secretary. Because what followed was an explosion in business unlike anything Wheeler had ever experienced in his life.

Signing Bernardi Electronics was like a catalyst. Once he secured that multimillion-dollar business's account, everything, *everything,* fell right into place. His creativity rebounded. His activity multiplied. His productivity soared. Opportunity knocked, over and over again, bringing with it a prosperity he never could have imagined in such a short span of time.

To put it in the vernacular, Rush Commercial Designs, Inc. thrived like a big dog. One local business after another lined up to hire Wheeler. Within a month he was able to recall his two former associates. And when he contacted Rosalie, his former secretary, at the end of that second month, he discovered, much to his good fortune, that she was available to return. It was as if all the planets had aligned and thrust the universe into total harmony, just for him. Once again Wheeler was in business, complete with a competent staff.

And a competent staff, he knew, was long overdue. Because although Audrey certainly kept up with the increased pace of the office, she was still very, very…well…Audrey.

Meaning that by June the coffee stains on Wheeler's rugs had multiplied in direct relation to the added workload. Of course by now he could afford to have someone come in weekly to clean, but that was beside the point—he was still cautious enough that he didn't want to fall into a pattern of unnecessary spending. His files, now housed in shiny new cabinets, fattened, but remained "organized" in as befuddling a manner as ever. Office machinery still broke on an almost daily basis, and although now there was a technician on retainer to attend to the problems, Wheeler again was concerned about the cost, even if it seemed negligible.

He simply did not want to overspend, as he had in the beginning.

Caution. That was the buzzword that flashed at the forefront of Wheeler's brain every single day. He wanted to be as careful as he could be not to plunge the business into dire straits again. And where Audrey Finnegan was concerned, dire straits were a way of life.

He liked Audrey—probably more than was wise—but where she was concerned, each day brought with it another minor, or sometimes major, catastrophe. He had been able to tolerate her mishaps in the beginning, because quite frankly he hadn't been able to afford *not* to tolerate them. Besides, his business had been failing then, so it hadn't seemed too serious a problem for his secretary to be one walking, talking accident waiting to happen. At that point her mishaps had been small indeed compared to the big picture.

But Rush Commercial Designs, Inc. was playing with the big boys now. Wheeler had entered the fast lane at an accelerated clip, and he wanted to make sure he avoided becoming roadkill again. With each added account came some new potential for disaster where Audrey was concerned. Although his clients liked her—she was, after all, quite charming and warm and sweet and cute and wonderful and...everything—she simply wasn't the kind of secretary a man in Wheeler's newly successful position should have.

He needed someone who could type *more* than seventeen words per minute. He needed someone who knew how to open a computer file without crashing the entire system. He needed someone who didn't file a design for Perfect Unions Dating Service under *H* for *hook-up.* He needed someone who didn't break things or injure herself and others on a regular basis. He needed someone who, quite frankly, had some inkling what the commercial design business was all about. And dammit, he needed—and deserved—someone who could make a decent cup of coffee.

Even though Wheeler had been telling himself these things for weeks—ever since it had become clear that the business was recovering to full capacity and then some— it was difficult for him to work up the nerve to tell Audrey their time together had come to an end. He stayed up all night writing a glowing reference for her to take back to One-Day-at-a-Timers Temp Service. And in addition to two weeks' severance pay—which he was in no way obligated to give her, seeing as how she wasn't, technically, his employee, nor was she, technically, being fired—he added a hefty bonus.

All that was left was to tell Audrey how much he'd appreciated her services, how very important she had been to the recovery of Rush Commercial Designs, Inc., and how much he would miss her smiling face and cheery show tunes around the office after she was gone. So, come Friday afternoon, as she was gathering her things and shutting down her work space for the day, he called her into his office.

When she entered, though, Wheeler almost chickened out. With the warmer weather, her outfits had become, if possible, even briefer and more revealing, and the sleeveless, bright turquoise sheath that she wore was complemented by, inescapably, all the turquoise accouterments necessary to make Audrey Finnegan, well...turquoise. Even the Band-Aid adhered to her left knee was bright blue. She had taken to wearing her hair down since that night at her...*lately,* he amended quickly, and the dark curls bounced riotously about her shoulders, spilling down her back in a tangle.

She looked fresh and sweet and inviting, and something inside him began to hum happily at the sight of her. In that moment Wheeler tried desperately to talk himself out of doing what he was about to do. Thankfully, however, good sense prevailed over the yearnings of his heart. With a quick request that she close the door behind her, he asked her to sit down and told her they had something they needed to talk about.

She looked understandably concerned at his request—because surely that wasn't resignation he saw in her expression. Still, she did as he asked, unavoidably tripping over the edge of the rug as she stepped forward, recovering as gracefully as someone cursed for life could, before seating herself in the chair he'd indicated.

He rose and rounded the front of his desk, then pushed himself up to sit atop it. Casual, he told himself. He must remember to keep it light and casual, even if light and casual were the last things he felt at the prospect of losing Audrey Finnegan.

"Audrey," he began, congratulating himself for managing what sounded like a carefree tone of voice, when thoughts were ricocheting through his head at an alarming speed. "I think you probably know what this is about."

She shook her head slightly, lifting her eyebrows a bit in expectation, and he suspected that no, she had no idea what this was about at all.

Dammit.

He swallowed hard before continuing. "Audrey," he said again, "you've been an invaluable asset to Rush Commercial Designs for the past two months, and I don't know that I could ever thank you enough for your part in helping me rebuild my business."

She narrowed her eyes at him. "I hear a big 'but' coming," she said.

He nodded, biting his lip at her phrasing. He felt like a big butt at the moment. "Yes," he said. "You do. You've been wonderful," he reiterated, "but I think the business has reached a point now where I'm going to need a secretary who has a broader knowledge of the business. Someone who would be a fuller partner in Rush Commercial

Designs. Someone who has a more complete understanding of the kind of detail work that goes into this kind of business. Someone who——''

"Someone who doesn't break things all the time," she finished for him with a smile that was sad and resigned. "Someone who doesn't spill coffee and fall down and make the office equipment explode."

Strangely there was no venom, no rancor, underscoring her words. Just a melancholy kind of understanding that this had been coming for a while now.

"Audrey, I——"

"That's okay," she interrupted. "Really. You don't owe me an explanation. For one thing, I'm a temp. I came to work for you knowing I'd only be here for as long as you needed me." She sighed heavily as she shrugged. "For another thing, to be perfectly honest, I'm amazed you didn't let me go a long time ago. Right after, oh, say…I fell on top of you that first day."

He smiled as he remembered. "As much as I've enjoyed working with you, Audrey, and as helpful as you've been, I really do need someone who knows a bit more about commercial design working for me. It's as simple as that."

She nodded, but he could tell she didn't believe him. "Thanks," she said as she stood. "It's nice of you to say so."

He remembered then that he had something to give her, so he, too, stood, snatching a legal-size envelope from his desk. He extended it toward her, but she didn't take it right away.

"It's a letter for One-Day-at-a-Timers," he told her. "Telling them how pleased I was with your performance."

She nodded again, but her smile wasn't quite in it. "Thanks," she mumbled as she took the envelope from him. "I appreciate it. I don't think I've ever had a nice reference from a former employer before."

He started to say more, but honestly had no idea what

WELCOME TO THE
CASINO!
Try your luck at the Roulette Wheel ...
Play a hand of Twenty-One!

How to play:

1. Play the Roulette and Twenty-One scratch-off games, as instructed on the opposite page, to see that you are eligible for FREE BOOKS and a FREE GIFT!

2. Send back the card and you'll receive TWO brand-new Silhouette Desire® novels. These books have a cover price of $3.75 each in the U.S. and $4.25 each in Canada, but they are yours to keep absolutely free.

3. There's no catch. You're under no obligation to buy anything. We charge nothing — ZERO — for your first shipment. And you don't have to make any minimum number of purchases — not even one!

4. The fact is, thousands of readers enjoy receiving books by mail from the Silhouette Reader Service™ before they're available in stores. They like the convenience of home delivery, and they love our discount prices!

5. We hope that after receiving your free books you'll want to remain a subscriber. But the choice is yours — to continue or cancel, any time at all!

So why not take us up on our invitation, with no risk of any kind. You'll be glad you did!

Play Twenty-One For This Exquisite Free Gift!

THIS SURPRISE
MYSTERY GIFT
WILL BE YOURS
FREE WHEN YOU PLAY
TWENTY-ONE

It's fun, and we're giving away *FREE GIFTS* to all players!

PLAY ROULETTE!

Scratch the silver to see that the ball has landed on 7 RED, making you eligible for TWO FREE romance novels!

PLAY TWENTY-ONE!

Scratch the silver to reveal a winning hand! Congratulations, you have Twenty-One. Return this card promptly and you'll receive a fabulous free mystery gift, along with your free books!

YES!

Please send me all the free Silhouette Desire® books and the gift for which I qualify! I understand that I am under no obligation to purchase any books, as explained on the back of this card.

Name: _____

(PLEASE PRINT)

Address: _____ Apt.#: _____

City: _____ State: _____ Zip: _____

The Silhouette Reader Service™ — Here's how it works:

Accepting your 2 free books and mystery gift places you under no obligation to buy anything. You may keep the books and gift and return the shipping statement marked "cancel." If you do not cancel, about a month later we'll send you 6 additional novels and bill you just $3.12 each in the U.S., or $3.49 each in Canada, plus 25¢ delivery per book and applicable taxes if any.* That's the complete price and — compared to the cover price of $3.75 in the U.S. and $4.25 in Canada — it's quite a bargain! You may cancel at any time, but if you choose to continue, every month we'll send you 6 more books, which you may either purchase at the discount price or return to us and cancel your subscription.

*Terms and prices subject to change without notice. Sales tax applicable in N.Y. Canadian residents will be charged applicable provincial taxes and GST.

BUSINESS REPLY MAIL

FIRST-CLASS MAIL   PERMIT NO 717   BUFFALO NY

POSTAGE WILL BE PAID BY ADDRESSEE

SILHOUETTE READER SERVICE
3010 WALDEN AVE
PO BOX 1867
BUFFALO NY 14240-9952

NO POSTAGE
NECESSARY
IF MAILED
IN THE
UNITED STATES

If offer card is missing write to: Silhouette Reader Service, 3010 Walden Ave., P.O. Box 1867, Buffalo, NY 14240-9952 would make this easier for either of them. He was surprised at the depth of his disappointment at having to let her go. Everything within him rebelled at the very idea of not having Audrey around anymore. Only now was he beginning to realize how much he had come to look forward to seeing her every morning. To chatting with her every afternoon. To simply being close to her on a day-to-day basis.

But what else could he do? He absolutely had to have someone competent in her position. And in her position as secretary, Audrey was in no way competent.

So he simply nodded toward the envelope in her hand and concluded as quickly as he could, "And, um…there's a little something in there for you, too."

She narrowed her eyes in confusion. "What do you mean?"

He sliced a hand through the air, suddenly feeling impatient for some reason. "Just something extra. A little bonus from me to say thank you, that's all."

Her mouth rounded into a perfect, red, luscious O. Then, as if that weren't quite enough to illustrate her thoughts, she stated aloud, "Oooh. I get it. Money, right?"

He nodded quickly, again feeling an odd irritation whose origin he couldn't understand. The bonus had seemed like a good idea at the time, a nice gesture to let her know how much she'd meant to him during her time at the office. Now, however, for some reason, giving Audrey money felt wrong. Almost tawdry.

He couldn't imagine why he would feel that way. It wasn't like the two of them had had a sexual relationship and now he was paying her off to make a clean break of it. Except for that one night at her apartment, they'd scarcely touched each other. Well, unless he included all those occasions when he caught her as she fell, which, granted, were numerous—and sometimes kind of intimate in an awkward sort of way. Still, the two of them had certainly never *actually* been intimate.

Unless, of course, he counted all those times they'd had sex in his imagination. Which, now that he made a quick mental tally, pretty much made them celebrating their seventy-fifth wedding anniversary when compared to the activity of other couples.

So, okay, maybe he'd given Audrey more than an occasional, scarce thought over the past couple of months, he conceded now. So sue him. Hey, he was a healthy, red-blooded male, and she was a healthy, uh…embodiment of everything a red-blooded male wanted in a female.

They hadn't had sex anywhere other than in his fantasies, he reminded himself, wondering why he suddenly felt so defensive. Even if in his fantasies they'd pretty much covered the gamut of locales, both mundane and exotic—his desk, her desk, his design table, the rug amid the coffee stains, the copy machine, the washroom off his office, the washroom at the end of the hall out front, every stick of furniture she possessed at her apartment, every square inch of his place.

And okay, so maybe every now and then, his imagination had really gotten the better of him, and they'd made love in the surf in some secluded Caribbean bay, or in the first-class section of a jumbo jet, or in the cockpit of a racing yacht, or in the rear seat of a roller coaster—boy, that had been a really good one—under the table at a variety of local eateries, and, lest he forget, which he never, ever would, in a hang glider taking off from the tallest peak in—

"But then, I guess that's not too surprising that you would think that," Audrey said, interrupting what had become a pretty nice recap of his rich fantasy life over the past couple of months.

Only then did he realize that she had been speaking for some time and he'd heard not a word of what she'd said. He gazed at her for a moment in confusion, then shook his head soundly to relieve it of all those graphic, explicit, hot, carnal, sexual…where was he? Oh, yeah. To rid it of all those unspeakably erotic, though never quite satisfying, daydreams.

Then he looked at her as levelly as he dared, considering the fact that he'd just spent the last few moments imagining her naked limbs entwined with his own, and said, "What did you say? I'm sorry, I was thinking about something else."

When she met his gaze, two bright spots of pink appeared on her cheeks, and somehow he got the feeling that she knew exactly what he'd been thinking about, and that might have been because she'd been thinking something along the same lines herself.

"Ah..." she began eloquently. "Never mind. It wasn't important."

She shifted the envelope from one hand to the other, never quite looking at it. Instead, she gazed solemnly at Wheeler, and he experienced the strangest sensation—that his heart weighed several pounds more than usual.

"Well," she said, turning her body slightly toward the door. As if it might hasten her progress, she jutted a thumb over her shoulder in that direction, as well. But she didn't move any closer to the exit, only stood there looking at Wheeler as if she were waiting for him to say more. Then, when it became evident he would not, she added, "Thanks. For everything."

"You're welcome," he rejoined. He, too, felt as if he should add something more, but he couldn't imagine what that might be. Unless it was just, "And thank *you*, too. For everything."

"Don't mention it."

He nodded, taking her at her word, remaining silent after that.

With one final, not-quite-genuine smile, Audrey turned and made her way to the door. He watched her go, all the while telling himself to say something more, anything that would get her to turn around again, just for one more glimpse of her face and her smile. But she kept walking and didn't glance back once, not even when she tripped over the fringe on the rug before passing through the door and closing it behind her.

Wheeler didn't alter his pose in the slightest for a full five minutes after her departure, somehow thinking that maybe if he didn't move, nothing in his office would change. But of course that was ridiculous. The moment Audrey left, everything changed. He tried to assure himself that that was the whole point, that in relieving her of her duties, it would make things run more professionally, more easily, more efficiently. But he didn't quite feel the surge of optimism he knew he should feel.

For some reason, the office seemed quieter now, he marveled, even though there was really no change in that regard. It was early Friday evening, and everyone had gone home, just as they did every Friday evening, so of course it was quiet in the office. It was always quiet this time of day when Wheeler was here alone. But somehow that aloneness suddenly seemed more solitary than it had before. More complete. More permanent.

Ridiculous, he told himself as he pushed off of his desk, gathered his things, and began his own end-of-the-day ritual before going home. The removal of one employee—a temporary employee, at that—did not make an office turn bleak. On the contrary, in this case, the removal of that one employee would improve things enormously. With Rosalie back in charge as queen, the office would hum with the efficiency of a beehive.

He was just missing Audrey because he had liked her as a person, Wheeler thought. And hey, there was no law that said he couldn't call her now, and ask her out in a more personal capacity. In fact, maybe he'd do just that. Now that she wasn't working for him, there wouldn't be that awkward boss/secretary thing going on between them that had hampered their personal relationship before, at least where Wheeler was concerned. With any luck at all, they might even wind up fulfilling that roller-coaster fantasy of his.

But as he locked up the office and began walking down Main Street toward Luigi's for a bite to eat, Wheeler knew that he probably wouldn't be calling Audrey to ask her out. In fact, he wouldn't be calling *any* woman to ask her out. He was still a very busy man, and would have his work cut out for him for some time, to ensure his business stayed firmly entrenched in the upper echelon where it had landed. That meant his days and nights and weekends all were going to be filled with work. He still didn't have time right now in his life to nurture a budding relationship with a woman—any woman.

And even if he did, Audrey was a woman who would command far more time and attention and patience than the average woman did. Because Audrey Finnegan was—he might as well just say it—*jinxed*. In a big, big way.

And there was no way to get around that particular phenomenon. She had worked for Wheeler for two months, and her luck during that time had never improved. She had remained unfortunate, clumsy, and pretty much hexed. She was, quite simply, one of those people who was cursed for life, to whom ill fortune attached itself with utter glee, for whatever reason that might be. Maybe it was by accident of birth, maybe it was bad karma, maybe it was negative energy, maybe it was payback for crimes committed in a previous life. Perhaps she was just a cosmic magnet for misfortune.

Whatever.

She was under a cloud and down at the heels, ill-fated and star-crossed, calamitous and disastrous, hapless and luckless. And now that Wheeler's life was finally back on track, the last thing he wanted to invite back into it was a walking, talking streak of bad luck.

So he wouldn't be calling Audrey Finnegan. As nice and

as sweet as she was, as beautiful and as sexy as she was, only a madman would knowingly commit the kind of mayhem that she represented. Wheeler's fortune was looking up, way up. No way was he going to mess with his good luck now.

What Wheeler didn't count on, or perhaps what he forgot, was that luck was a capricious little beggar who took no prisoners. Unfortunately this was something of which he was brutally reminded less than a month after Audrey's departure from his life. And he was reminded of it in more ways than one.

The emptiness he'd begun to feel immediately after she left his office that day only grew larger and more unmanageable, until he felt like he was just one, big gaping wound. He missed her chirpy greetings in the morning, missed the smile that never failed to stir him out of whatever funk he had fallen into. He missed trying to guess what color she'd be on any given day, missed trying to predict on what part of her person she'd have the inescapable Band-Aid. Hell, he'd even begun to miss the rocket fuel she passed off as coffee. Simply put, he missed *her*.

But what was just as bad as the vacancy he felt in his heart whenever he thought about Audrey, was the fact that shortly after her departure, his business started to fall once again into decline. No sooner had he realigned his staff, his business, his life and his planets, than all hell broke loose and sent everything back into a turmoil.

His clients quickly became disenchanted. His staff quickly became surly. His secretary, who had reacted to Audrey's filing system in a way that was, shall we say, very bad, quickly became homicidal. Wheeler himself quickly became terrified that history was about to repeat itself. And for the life of him, he couldn't figure out why it was happening.

It made no sense. He'd gone over it and over it, around

and around and around, trying to figure out where, exactly, things had started to go wrong. But no matter how he looked at it, no matter which direction he approached it from, he could find no reason for the complete and seemingly irreversible downturn. He'd done nothing differently over the last month than he'd been doing before. But the last time he could remember things going well had been—

Right before he gave Audrey her walking papers.

Oh, no. Surely not…

His thoughts were thankfully interrupted by the quick rap of knuckles against his office door. Before he could even call out an invitation to enter, the door burst open and Rosalie strode through, her eyes flashing with purpose, her stride meaningful. Without a word, she crossed the office to Wheeler's desk, where she silently slapped down a sheet of Rush Commercial Designs, Inc. letterhead upon which was typed two words:

I quit.

He glanced up at her in alarm. "What the hell is this?"

"My resignation," she stated flatly, hands fisted on her ample hips.

"What? You can't resign. I just hired you back a month ago."

"I'm sorry, Wheeler," she said without an ounce of apology, "but I can't work under these conditions. Those files are *never* going to make sense, the computer does things now even a demonic possession wouldn't make it do, and, quite frankly, I'm sick of trying to make sense of it all. Read my lips. I quit."

Wheeler stood, extending his hands helplessly toward her. "Rosalie, you can't quit. I need you right now."

"I'll say you do," she assured him. "Not only is Rupert Skolnik on the warpath, but Charles Bernardi has been gunning for you all week. And don't even get me started on that whole Windsor Deli fiasco."

Wheeler dropped back into his chair with barely restrained panic, feeling as limp and unloved as an ugly rag doll. "Keep putting Bernardi off," he said. "I just need another day or two before I can go over that new project with him. Put them all off. Just for a few more days. That's all I ask. And don't quit. Things will go back to normal, Rosalie, you'll see. I just need a little time."

"You put them off," she countered. "I don't work here anymore."

"Rosalie, please…"

"And you'd better be careful, because Stephen and Sondra are making noises about quitting, too."

His associates. God, not them, as well. Was everyone going to abandon ship on him?

"Look, Rosalie, I know things seem a little chaotic now, but we'll recover from this. I know we will. Just give it a little time."

She met his gaze levelly. "No offense, Wheeler, but that's what you said the last time and look what happened."

He swallowed hard. He'd rather not look at what happened last time, thank you very much. He'd barely pulled out of that slump. The only thing that had saved him then had been—

Audrey's arrival.

Oh, no. Surely not…

"Rosalie, I promise—"

"I quit, Wheeler," she repeated. "I'm sorry, but I do. It's just not worth it. I can find work anywhere, and I won't have to undo all the damage created and all the havoc wreaked by former employees."

"Oh, come on, Rosalie, she wasn't that bad."

He wasn't sure why he rose so quickly to his extemporary secretary's defense, especially since he'd seen for himself that she could indeed wreak havoc like a pro. But suddenly Wheeler felt as if he had been cast in the role of Audrey's champion. And it ticked him off to hear someone impugn her abilities, even if those abilities were some-what impugnable.

The look his soon-to-be-ex-secretary gave him told him that she pretty much didn't believe his assurance. He wanted to argue, but it would have been pointless. Not just because Rosalie clearly had her mind made up about quit-ting, but also because she left then without saying another word, slamming the door hard behind her, something that rather hampered the effectiveness of any argument Wheeler might want to offer.

He fell back into his chair, folded his elbows onto his desk, dumped his head into his hands and raked his fingers through his dark hair. Why was this happening to him? he wondered. Why had everything gone to hell in a handbasket this way? What had he done wrong to make things turn sour so completely, with such devastation? There was ab-solutely nothing different now from what had been there a month ago, when the sudden shift had begun. Nothing had changed in the month since Audrey had left. Nothing ex-cept—

Audrey.

Oh, no. Surely not…

But the more Wheeler thought about it, the more he ar-rived at the same conclusion. No matter which way he tried to steer his arguments, they always arrived at the same destination. They always stopped at Audrey Finnegan.

Shortly after she had arrived in his life, his business had begun to turn around. Right after that near-hit romantic interlude at her apartment, his business had begun to ex-plode. As long as Audrey had been working for him, ev-erything had been rosy and bright and prosperous. The closer they'd come to each other, in fact, the faster business had picked up. And right after he'd let her go, his business had rapidly begun to decline.

Audrey. No matter which way he went, there she was. It all circulated around Audrey Finnegan. It all coincided

with her coming into and going out of his life. As long as
he'd had her by his side, literally as well as figuratively,
everything had gone swimmingly.

Good heavens. Despite the fact that she could have been
the poster child for Misfortune International, she had been
his good-luck charm all along.

He'd halfway joked about that from the beginning, but
that's all it had been—a joke. For anyone to think someone
like Audrey could actually bring good luck, well… That
was just crazy. There was nothing fortunate about the
woman at all.

Except where Wheeler was concerned.

He told himself he was being crazy, that there was no
such thing as a good-luck charm. People made their own
luck, good or bad, and keeping a person or object close by
had nothing to do with how well one performed.

He told himself he was being pathetic, that this was simply the reaction of a desperate man, one who was grasping
at whatever foolhardy explanation he could find to account
for a sudden professional downturn.

He told himself he was being silly, thinking Audrey Finnegan, of all people, would be responsible for his professional success, when she was the last person on the planet
who might inspire feelings of good fortune.

But he was a crazy, pathetic, silly man who was about
to suffer a disastrous professional downfall if he didn't do
something quick to turn things around. At this point even
hiring back Audrey Finnegan was worth a shot. Hey, at this
point he'd invoke voodoo magic or offer up a pagan sac-
rifice if it meant putting his business back on track again.
Returning Audrey to the fold seemed in no way unreason-
able.

He had to get her back. Whatever it took, Wheeler would
do it. Whatever she wanted, he'd give it to her. No matter
where she was or what she was doing, she had to stop doing
it and come back to work for him. He didn't care how many

coffee stains he had to clean up or how many new office machines he had to buy. He needed Audrey back. Desperately. Otherwise...

Otherwise, his luck was going to run out.

Seven

Audrey giggled softly as she rinsed the shampoo from Rex's long, silky, golden hair. She nuzzled the firm muscles beneath his warm, soapy shoulder, cooed seductive words into his ear and lovingly massaged his back to soothe away all the day's stresses. In response, he gazed longingly back at her with those velvety chocolate-brown eyes of his and sighed with much contentment.

He was the perfect male, she thought with a smile. So handsome. So strong. So sweet. So smart. And she knew he would do anything for her if she but asked. Now if she could just do something about his breath....

Ah, well, she reasoned philosophically. You couldn't have everything. Besides, what else could you expect from a golden retriever?

The big dog's tongue lolled out the side of his mouth then, making Audrey laugh. Working as a dog groomer wasn't without its perks, she thought. She'd made some really good friends since coming to work at what the owner of the establishment termed a "canine salon." Of course, all those new friends had four legs, bad breath and conversational skills limited to the words *woof* and *grrr* and the odd howl, but that was a vocabulary more extensive than some of her ex-boyfriends claimed.

She'd lost her job with One-Day-at-a-Timers almost immediately after beginning her new assignment for a local bank, because she'd crashed their computer system in a big way. The good news was that in doing so, she had pretty much wiped out the national debt. The bad news was, it was only on paper. The bad news was also that the bank manager had to be tranquilized at the scene, and the paramedics had sort of thought it might be better if Audrey just took her leave quietly then, before anybody else got hurt.

It was just as well, she thought now. Ever since her job at Rush Commercial Designs, Inc. had come to an end a month before, her heart hadn't been in her temp work, anyway. And she was beginning to think she might have finally found her niche as a dog groomer. The animals loved her, and she was getting especially good at canine pedicures.

Best of all, in the two weeks that she'd been working at Scruff E. Neck's, she hadn't made one single mistake. Well, none that mattered, anyway. Much. As long as she stayed away from the cash register and the blow dryer. And the light switches and the refrigerator. And the power vacuum and the electric clippers. And pretty much all of the other appliances, too. As long as she did that, everything was fine.

The only thing she felt bad about these days was the fact that Wheeler Rush was no longer a part of her daily routine. She missed him. A lot. She missed seeing him all pressed and starched every day at his desk. She missed the soft murmur of his voice on the other side of his office door whenever he'd been on the telephone. She missed his smiles, his shrugs, his sighs. She even missed the barely restrained exasperation in his voice whenever he'd said, "No problem, Audrey. Honest."

And at night when she was lying alone in bed, she could never quite fight off the memory of that one delicious evening the two of them had spent together socially. She recalled in vivid detail what they'd eaten for dinner, what they'd talked about on the walk home, and, it went without saying, what had happened on her sofa right after her cats had tried to cripple Wheeler for life.

In many ways Audrey wondered if she would ever quite be able to forget about that one incident with him. Because even though it had happened months ago, just thinking about it now could still raise her temperature to dangerous levels. And she couldn't help but wonder what might have happened if she'd just kept her mouth shut that night and let things move along to their natural conclusion.

In fact, so often did she think about Wheeler, that once or twice she'd picked up her telephone with the intention to call him, just to say hello and see how he was doing. But she'd stopped herself before punching the last number, because she just wasn't comfortable calling a guy on the phone. Especially a guy who she'd spilled coffee on—repeatedly. And whose office equipment she'd destroyed—on more than one occasion. And whose legs had nearly been broken by her cats. And whose spare change of clothes she'd never returned.

Even so, there had been one day when she'd stopped by his office because she'd been downtown anyway, shopping at the Galleria. She'd thought she would just run in to offer a quick "Hi" and "'Bye" and refill her soul with the sight and smell and sound of him. But he'd been out at the time, and she hadn't left a message with the too, too efficient secretary seated at Audrey's desk. Or, rather, Audrey's ex-desk. She supposed it had never really been hers to begin with. She'd only been temporary, after all.

In more ways than one, evidently.

The bell out in the lobby jangled then, signaling the arrival at Scruff E. Neck's of another pet owner in dire need of pet maintenance. Quickly Audrey finished towel drying Rex and led him back to his kennel. Then she hastily swiped her hands over the long, red apron covering her hot-pink jeans and hot-pink T-shirt, tossed her ponytail back over her shoulder and went out to greet the arrival.

She was more than a little surprised to see that it was Wheeler Rush. Not just because she had been thinking about him mere seconds ago, but also because she hadn't realized he had any pets.

"Hi," she said with a smile, feeling a familiar warmth spread easily through her entire body at the sight of him. He smiled back in response, and, just like that, that easy warmth became a full-fledged forest fire. *Wow.*

"Hi, yourself," he said.

She glanced down at his side, but saw no sign of pet activity. "What are you doing here?" she asked as she returned her gaze to his face.

He didn't answer right away. For a long moment he only gazed back at her, staring first at her eyes, then her hair, then her mouth. His gaze swept down the front of her, then back up again, before settling once more on her mouth. But his expression revealed nothing of what he might be thinking. Audrey's heart beat rapid-fire in response to his inspection, and she wondered what was going through his mind as he studied her.

He was probably thinking that she looked and smelled like someone who had been shampooing dogs all day. But what did he expect? she thought further, feeling unaccountably irritated by his reaction. She *had* been shampooing dogs all day. Hey, if he wanted someone who smelled like a rose, then he should have hired a gardener in the first place. So there.

And why were her thoughts so frazzled and bizarre all

of a sudden? Maybe because her entire body was so frazzled and bizarre all of a sudden.

"I came for you, Audrey."

His words, uttered with such clarity, such possession, such certainty, ignited little fires throughout her entire system, fires that leaped and danced and spread—quickly. Because the look in his eyes when he spoke them was absolutely—

Oh, boy.

"Uh," she said. "What was that? I...I think I must have misunderstood you."

He chuckled a little bit, but still seemed kind of anxious. "I came for you," he repeated.

This time, though, the announcement didn't sound quite so adamant as it had the first time. On the contrary, he suddenly sounded almost worried about something.

"I almost panicked when I called One-Day-at-a-Timers," he rushed on, "and they told me you weren't employed there anymore. I thought I'd lost you forever."

Her heart began to slam against her rib cage at the ease with which he delivered his concern. He was worried about losing her forever? she thought. But...nobody was worried about losing her forever.

"So how did you find me, then?" she asked.

His eyes fairly sparkled as he looked at her. "I went to your apartment this afternoon, to see you, but you weren't there. Your downstairs neighbor, Mrs.... Mrs. somebody..."

"Mrs. Wendover," Audrey said automatically.

"Right. Mrs. Wendover told me you were working here."

"She's a regular here. She has two shih tzus."

"Gesundheit," he said with a smile.

She smiled back. Oh, yeah. She'd missed him. A lot. "Thanks," she said softly.

"You're welcome. Anyway, I needed to find you."

"Why?" she asked again.

"Because I need you, Audrey," he said unabashedly. Then, seeming to realize how his remark might be misconstrued, he hastened to clarify, "At work, I mean. I need you to come back to work at your old job. At Rush Commercial Designs."

She narrowed her eyes at him, marveling at his uncanny ability to make her fantasies come true. Ever since she'd started working at Scruff E. Neck's, she'd enjoyed one daydream after another about how Wheeler Rush would come striding into the canine salon one sunny morning, drop to his knees and beg her to return to him because he needed her desperately.

Okay, so maybe she hadn't fantasized him needing her for her secretarial nonskills, as he was now, but still... There was something way too déjà vu-ey about this whole scenario.

"You need me to come back to work for you?" she echoed, still certain she must be misunderstanding.

He nodded.

"Why?" she asked again.

He opened his mouth to answer, then, evidently not knowing exactly what to say, closed it. Audrey took it to be not a good sign.

"I mean, don't get me wrong," she started again, "but we both know I wasn't the greatest secretary in the world, and you were so gung-ho to hire back your old secretary once you could afford to. And then there's that small matter of me falling all the time and me spilling coffee all the time and me breaking everything I came into contact with and me not knowing what I was doing most of the time and—"

"Oh, that," he interrupted her easily.

Oh, that?

He shoved his hands deep into the pockets of his dark trousers. Then, clearly restless, he withdrew them and fiddled with the knot in his multicolored necktie. Then he smoothed a nonexistent wrinkle out of his white dress shirt. His gaze darted around the lobby as he continued, "Well, yes, but…um… Those things…they're, uh…"

"Yeah?"

His gaze finally found its way back to her face, then flitted off again. "Well, none of that is essential for a good secretary," he said.

"It's not?"

He shook his head. "No, of course not."

"You don't think it's important that a secretary have some, oh…I don't know…basic secretarial skills?"

"Absolutely not."

"I see."

She didn't know why she was arguing with him, when everything he was saying was what she'd been wanting to hear for a month now. She ought to just jump at his offer and trot right back downtown with him and take up where they'd left off. The thing was Audrey just wasn't really sure precisely where they'd left off. Just what exactly was inspiring Wheeler's offer of reemployment?

"Well," she said cautiously, "if what you're looking for is a secretary who doesn't have any basic skills or abilities of any kind, then I guess I'm definitely the woman you need."

He smiled with what was obvious relief. "Can you start tomorrow?"

She gaped at him. "Tomorrow? But I really should give two weeks' notice here," she said. "It wouldn't be polite to just up and quit like that. Mr. Easley needs me."

"Two weeks?" Wheeler repeated incredulously. "You won't be available for *two weeks*? But anything could happen between now and then."

Goodness, but he was anxious to get her back. Could it be at all possible that his need for her went beyond the professional? Did she dare hope that? "Well, maybe I could make it in one week," she amended.

He didn't seem to be at all appeased by her offer. "Look, if I can find someone to fill in for you here until your required time is up, will you come back to work for me tomorrow?"

She arched her brows in surprise. "Yeah, sure, I guess so. If Mr. Easley says it's okay."

Wheeler nodded. "Consider it done. My niece, Wendy, has been looking for a summer job, and she's great with animals." He inhaled a deep breath and expelled it slowly, as if he were trying to slow his heart rate. "Then you'll be at your desk tomorrow morning? Bright and early? I can count on seeing you there?"

His voice had taken on an almost desperate edge by now, and Audrey couldn't help but be amazed by it. Just what was going on? Had he really missed her that much? Was she really that important to him? And if so, then in exactly what way?

"Wheeler?" she said tentatively.

"Yes?"

She needed to get something straight before she could fully commit to her return. So, choosing her words carefully, she asked, "Why do you want me to come back? Really, I mean?"

He started to reply immediately, and she could see by his expression that it was going to be another one of those lame platitudes that were so clearly untrue. She was *not* a good secretary. There was no point in her thinking otherwise. And she had *not* been an asset to his company. There was no way he would ever convince her that he wanted her back because of her professional attributes. Simply put, she didn't *have* any professional attributes. At least not where any secretarial skills were concerned.

So she held up a hand, palm out, to stop him before he could say another word about talents that she didn't possess. "Tell me truthfully," she insisted. "I know it's not because I'm efficient or knowledgeable about commercial design or whatever. I know it's not my secretarial ability you've missed. So be honest with me, Wheeler. Why do you want me to come back to work for you? Really.''

Once again he drew a deep, thoughtful breath, expelling it in another slow, steady sigh. Then, his gaze fixed levelly on hers, he told her, ''Rosalie quit on me.''

Audrey nodded in understanding, her heart sinking at the realization that he would only come looking for her when he was desperate to replace his first choice.

''But that's not the only reason,'' he rushed on. ''I've missed you, Audrey. A lot. The office hasn't been the same with you gone.''

That was only marginally better, she thought. That he wanted her back because he was feeling nostalgic. Nostalgic for weird stuff, too, seeing as how she'd made his life more than a little difficult when she'd worked for him before.

Seeming to read her thoughts, he added, ''And my life hasn't been the same without you, either.''

Okay, so that showed some promise. ''What do you mean?'' she asked him.

''I mean...I've missed you,'' he repeated with a shrug. ''And I'd like to have you back. In my office. And in my life.''

She decided not to push her luck any more than she already had, and took his statement for what it was worth. Namely, something really vague. Vagueness was good, she told herself. She could do a lot with vagueness, and had on a number of occasions. Vagueness was workable.

''Okay,'' she said. ''If you can get your niece to cover for me, I'll be back at my desk tomorrow morning, bright and early.''

His entire body seemed to go limp at her assurance, and she marveled yet again at how desperately he seemed to want her back. No man had ever wanted Audrey in such a way. Ever. At best, her boyfriends had tolerated her. But Wheeler honestly seemed to want her. To need her. Badly.

Not that he was her boyfriend, she quickly corrected herself. Not by a long shot. But some of what he had said had been kind of personal. Sort of. In a way. Hadn't it? Or had she just imagined that part?

Audrey sighed, too, more fitfully than Wheeler had. It was going to be interesting, returning to work for Rush Commercial Designs, Inc. she thought. She just hoped she was up to the task.

Task, she repeated to herself with much disgust two weeks later as she tidied up her desk at the end of the day. What a laugh. *Task* suggested some small job that needed doing, like scrubbing the sink or vacuuming out the windowsills. What had met Audrey upon her return to Rush Commercial Designs, Inc., was a labor of Herculean proportions.

How had Wheeler and his staff managed to get along in her absence? she wondered, not for the first time. In an effort to economize and organize, all they'd managed to do was eradicate and obliterate.

First, some file fascist had come in and made a mess of Audrey's nicely arranged files to the point where they made no sense at all. Second, someone had reconfigured her computer so that everything was in columns and rows and stuff, and she'd had no idea where to look for *any*thing. Third, Wheeler's clients had been in total upheaval about too many things to name. And as if all that weren't enough, fourth—and this had been the most upsetting—they had switched brands of coffee.

Now, however, things were beginning to level out a bit. Oh, sure, there was still the occasional glitch in the system—what office didn't suffer those from time to time…or hour to hour. Whatever. Mostly, though, things were starting to run the way they had run when Audrey had worked for Wheeler the first time. And even though that meant there were still a number of crises to get through during the day, those crises had shrunk significantly in number, and they no longer seemed to consist of life-and-death—at least where the business was concerned—extremes.

She even got along with Wheeler's two associates better this time than she had the last, though they still weren't what you might call people people. Then again, Audrey was more careful what she said to them these days. Looking back to her previous stint at Rush Commercial Designs, Inc., she supposed asking Sondra how she liked her new Wonderbra that first day Sondra wore it hadn't been such a good idea. But, sheesh, it wasn't like it was any big secret or anything. A woman goes up two cup sizes overnight, it's kind of noticeable. And, looking back, too, Audrey probably shouldn't have offered that suggestion about Rogaine to Stephen, but honestly, men were just so sensitive about the whole hair thing.

Oh, well, she thought with a sigh now as she gathered up her things to go. The office and its staff were running much more efficiently this time around. At least she'd made it through two whole weeks without hurting herself. Well, without hurting herself *much,* she amended, gazing down at the bright green Band-Aid that spanned the back of her hand. And in that two weeks' time, she hadn't broken anything, either. Well, nothing *major,* she qualified, turning her attention to the digital clock on her desk that flashed 0:00 over and over again, making her feel like they were suddenly running on Armageddon time.

Still, all in all, it really was nice to be back.

"Audrey."

She spun around at Wheeler's summons, catching her foot on her chair as she did and falling back down into it. But at least this time she landed fanny first. Quickly she tugged her chartreuse minidress back into place and pretended she'd meant to sit down with her legs sprawled in that totally unprofessional way all along. She smiled nervously, holding back a sigh at the simple sight of her boss standing there framed by his office door.

Ever since her return, she had come to think of him as one of her perks. Now that she was considered a full-time employee, she actually received benefits. But full medical, dental *and* optical couldn't even come close to the simple pleasure of sharing the same roof with Wheeler Rush.

He looked as handsome as ever in his dark trousers and white dress shirt, his necktie loosened at his open collar. But his hair was mussed, as if he'd been grasping great, heaving handfuls of it in frustration all afternoon, and his eyes were smudged below by purple crescents.

He seemed so tired, she thought, so stressed out. She had run interference for him where his clients were concerned, and had managed to improve relations in most cases. So far no one had bailed out on him. But there were a couple of accounts that were still iffy. Audrey would work on them a little harder to make sure they stayed onboard. Whatever she had to do to make things easier for Wheeler, she would do it. Hey, that was her job, after all.

"Was there something you needed before I go home?" she asked.

He nodded wearily. "Yes, there is," he told her. "I need to tell you thanks for everything you've done over the past two weeks. It's really meant a lot to the business." His smile grew warmer, his eyes softer. "And it's meant a lot to me, too."

She smiled back, her heart purring with a rapid *pitty-pat, pitty-pat, pitty-pat* at the warm light flickering in his eyes. "Just doing my job," she said, voicing her thoughts out loud.

He nodded again, more thoughtfully this time. "Yes, you are doing that. Things have improved enormously since your return. I knew I needed you back. And you're working out exactly as I thought you would."

There was something kind of funny about the way he said that—and about the way he looked at her when he did, too—but Audrey couldn't quite put her finger on what it was. So she just chalked it up to his obvious fatigue and the general chaos of getting things back under control.

And then, before she could stop herself, she said, "You look awfully tired. You want to come over to my place for dinner tonight? It would save you having to fix something for yourself. And I could update you on some of your clients I spoke to today."

He didn't answer her right away, and instead gave her invitation some thought. Finally he nodded slowly. "Yeah. I think I'd like that a lot."

"It won't be anything fancy," she cautioned him. "But I could manage something decent, I think." She shrugged philosophically. "At least you won't have to cook it yourself."

He chuckled softly, halfheartedly, and again it struck her how hard he'd been working lately. "Give me ten minutes to wind a few things up," he said. "Then we can take my car."

That last part was superfluous, really, seeing as how Wheeler had been driving her home from work every night since she'd come back. He kept telling her it was because she only lived a couple of blocks away from him and that, seeing as how she was right on his way, there was no point in her waiting for the bus and taking twice as long to get home every night. But somehow Audrey had the feeling that the reason for his daily offers went beyond his simple Good Samaritan tendencies. For some reason she had the impression that he wanted to keep an eye on her.

She didn't know why that was, but no matter how hard she tried to shake the feeling, it stayed with her. Where before, it had always seemed as if Wheeler was trying to steer clear of her whenever she was about, now he seemed to be everywhere, always looking over her shoulder, always asking her if she needed anything, always wanting to be sure she was content in her position with the company. And all she could think was that he wanted to know where she was at any given moment, should he need her for...

Something. She just didn't know exactly what. But she definitely felt as if he considered her absolutely essential to his well-being. Now if she could just figure out precisely in what way, maybe she could go about reassuring him that she wasn't going anywhere.

In any case, something was different about Wheeler now, she thought as she watched him return to his office, leaving the door open in his wake. He wasn't the same boss she'd had when she'd worked for him as a temp. There was a desperation about him now that hadn't been there before, even when his business had been on its last legs. Certainly he'd had worries aplenty with the downturn he'd been suffering since her departure, she thought, but still...

It was just different, she thought again. He was more attentive, more needful, more insistent. It was almost as if he feared—truly, genuinely *feared*—losing her.

"All set?" he asked as he exited his office.

She forced a lighthearted smile and tried to tamp down all the strange sensations bubbling up inside her head and her heart. "I'm ready when you are."

He nodded once. "Great. But instead of you cooking, why don't we stop by Luigi's and get something to carry out? And we can hit Old Towne for a bottle of wine on the way to your place."

"Champagne," she said with a laugh, rising to precede him out. "To celebrate a great leveling-off period."

"And the good things to come," he added, following right behind her. "Because, Audrey, with you at my side, I'm confident there will only be good times ahead."

Eight

Wheeler gazed across the kitchen table at his good-luck charm and marveled again at what an amazingly fortunate man he was.

He was so lucky that Audrey had stumbled—quite literally, he recalled—into his life that first time, when his business had been just about to go belly-up. He was so lucky that he'd realized before it was too late how she had figured into the scheme of things by being his good-luck charm. He was so lucky that he'd found her a second time, when he'd feared she was gone forever. And he was so lucky that she liked working for him, enough that she would stay. At least, he hoped she liked working for him enough to stay. Because he didn't know what he would do without her.

Well, he'd lose his business, of that much he was certain. And if he lost his business, then everything else would fall apart right behind it.

Never mind that Audrey wasn't the most qualified secretary in the world. Never mind that he would probably spend the rest of his life replacing coffee makers and microwaves and computers. Never mind that, sooner or later, one or both of them was bound to end up in a hospital. Never mind that ideally Audrey was in no way the kind of woman he would normally employ.

As ill-fated as she was as a human being, she brought nothing but good fortune to Wheeler's life. That was all that mattered. She was his good-luck charm.

She really was. She'd only been back at Rush Commercial Designs for two weeks, but already he'd seen major changes in the business. His clients weren't gunning for him anymore. Some of them had actually apologized for ever doubting him. His creativity had returned in a massive outpouring of ideas. He'd even taken on a couple of new clients.

And it was all because of Audrey. He would never believe otherwise, because she was the only explanation that made any sense. Her arrival and departure and return to his life coincided specifically with the performance of his company and the blossoming of his brain. When she was working for him, his business boomed and his creativity bloomed. And when she was gone, his business went bust and his creativity hit a brick wall.

However it happened, she brought him good luck, and without her his luck ran out. It was that simple. Therefore Wheeler had to do whatever was necessary to make sure she never left him. Because without her in his life, and his office, he was destined for unthinkable doom.

"More coffee?" she asked suddenly.

Unprepared for the question, Wheeler automatically nodded, then immediately regretted his error as he watched the thick black substance ooze into his cup. "Uh, thank you," he said, pleased that he managed to do so without gagging.

"Anytime," she said with a smile before returning to her chair.

They'd finished with both dinner and topics of conversation some time ago, and Wheeler had helped her store the remnants and clean up the aftermath while the coffee was brewing. The early-summer sun was hanging low in the sky, marking the end of a long, long day. There was really no reason for him to hang around, he thought. Strangely, though, he found that he wanted to do just that. For as long as Audrey would allow.

The wine they'd enjoyed with dinner—chardonnay instead of champagne, because Wheeler didn't want to jinx his good luck by being overly confident, with or without Audrey—made him feel mellow. For the first time in more than a month he felt himself relaxing. His muscles weren't tense, his head wasn't pounding, his stomach wasn't churning. Instead, as he absorbed the sight of Audrey Finnegan seated across from him, an easy feeling of well-being filtered through him, settling in his bones and calming him beyond measure.

She had retreated to the bathroom to change her clothes while Wheeler set the table, and now she was wearing an oversize purple shirt of some light, breezy fabric and matching leggings. Her hair tumbled unfettered around her shoulders in a riot of curls, and her face was scrubbed free of makeup. She seemed more approachable now than she did at work, less a secretary—less even a good-luck charm—and more a woman.

Inevitably his thoughts returned to the last time he had passed the evening at her apartment. Of course, that wasn't unusual, seeing as how his thoughts had returned to that evening on an almost daily basis since it had happened. But always on those occasions, instead of recalling the way he and Audrey had actually parted that night, his traitorous brain managed to change the outcome significantly, so that they never parted at all.

Tonight was no different. As Wheeler sat there watching Audrey sip benignly from her cup, he envisioned them again entwined on the sofa, taking their exploration of each other considerably further than they had that night—and considerably further than would be prudent. Not just because he was her boss, and such a development would make for awkward working conditions. But also because she was his good-luck charm, and he couldn't risk losing her over some silly romantic entanglement gone sour.

Because anything romantic that might occur with Audrey would almost certainly go sour. As much as Wheeler needed her in his life for good luck, to involve himself too intimately with such an unfortunate woman would lead to disaster. Right now he was in no shape to undertake a romantic relationship with the ideal woman, let alone a woman like Audrey, with whom even a step in the wrong direction could prove disastrous.

She was totally jinxed, he reminded himself. Even if she was really cute and sweet and funny and sexy and…and everything, even if she did set in motion dreams and desires unlike anything he'd ever experienced before, even if she was responsible for him feeling just so damned good about everything, it simply would not be a good idea to get too deeply involved. No, it would be best if they just kept things platonic. And professional. And impersonal.

"I think Mrs. Tobias and Ms. Duran at the Megastar Corporation are coming around to your way of thinking on the new project you're doing for them."

Audrey's comment was exactly what Wheeler needed to bring his thoughts around. Professional. Impersonal. Yepper, that was what he needed right now. Anything to erase his current speculation about what she might—or might not—be wearing under that purple top of hers.

"Really?" he said, nudging his libido aside.

Regrettably his libido refused to be nudged, and instead rebounded quickly, pondering the question of whether Audrey's shoulders and back and belly were as soft and creamy as he suspected they were.

"They certainly are," she said.

Wheeler narrowed his eyes, wondering if he'd just spoken his thoughts aloud. "They are? Really?"

"Oh, absolutely," she assured him enthusiastically. "Those two women at Megastar think you're just the monkey's eyebrows."

Oh, that, he thought. "Uh…is that good?" he asked. "Being a monkey's eyebrow, I mean?"

"Trust me," she said with a knowing nod. "You're in like skin with them."

Surely he heard that wrong, he thought. "In like skin?" he repeated.

She looked at him as if he'd just grown a third arm. "No, I said, 'in like Flynn,'" she replied. "'In like skin' makes no sense."

"And 'monkey's eyebrows' does?"

"Sure. You've never heard that phrase?"

He shook his head. Would there ever come a time when Audrey Finnegan ceased to be a font of…of…of something really confusing to him?

"Oh," she said.

He sighed. "Well, in any event, if you say they're coming around, that's good enough for me."

It wasn't at all surprising that his clients were suddenly on his side. She was, after all, his good-luck charm. She made all the difference in the world.

"And I took care of all your travel arrangements for the Cincinnati conference next week," she added. "You sure you don't want me to go up there with you? It sounds like it's going to be pretty chaotic."

He shook his head. "No, thank you. It's not necessary. I'll be fine."

"I don't mind. It's just the weekend. And I don't have any other plans."

"No, really, Audrey. I'll be fine alone. Thank you."

He didn't even want to think about what a highway journey with the ill-fated Audrey Finnegan would be like. At best, there would doubtless be mechanical failure or a flat tire that required a dangerous roadside change. Or they'd end up in Nashville, Tennessee, instead of Cincinnati, Ohio. At worst…well, the traffic-fatality rate being what it was over the Fourth of July weekend, the worst didn't bear thinking about.

"Okay, but if you change your mind, I can be packed and ready to go in less than an hour."

He smiled. "You enjoy the long weekend here. I'll be fine," he reiterated.

She didn't look convinced of that, however, and gazed at him for a long time in silence, as if she had something on her mind that she wanted to say but was reluctant to voice.

"What?" he asked. "What is it?"

She opened her mouth to speak, then seemed to think better of the action and closed it again. But she continued to study him quite openly. Audrey had never been one for being able to keep her thoughts a secret, however. Wheeler knew her well enough by now to know that if she had something on her mind, sooner or later he'd find out about it. And when he did, it would almost certainly involve some kind of bodily pain or the loss of a prized memento.

This time it was to be sooner, he realized. Because she opened her mouth again and said, "Wheeler, I'm worried about you. You work too hard. You need to stop pushing yourself so much."

He supposed it wasn't such an unusual thing for a secretary to say to her boss. But there was something about the way Audrey said it that went way beyond the secretarial. And he told himself he really should put a stop to whatever that something was—immediately. It just wasn't a good idea to encourage a relationship between them that was anything other than professional. As much as he might want to.

"Audrey, everything is fine," he said, conjuring his most winning smile to convince her he was telling the truth. "Yes, everything in my life fell apart after you left, and I had a rough time of it while you were gone. But now that I have you back, everything is as it should be. You're all I needed to make everything perfect again."

It took Wheeler all of ten seconds to realize that he probably should have worded his reassurance a little differently. Because in those ten seconds, it became abundantly clear that Audrey had totally misinterpreted what he had said.

All he had wanted to do was tell her that she had become important to him. But it was quite obvious that Audrey thought he was telling her she had become, well, *important* to him. As something other than a secretary. As oh, say…a romantic interest. He sensed that immediately by the soft glow that warmed her face, by the shy smile that curled her lips and by the dewy shine that brightened her eyes.

And he also sensed it by the way she sighed and said, "Oh, Wheeler. I'm so happy you feel that way. Because I feel that way, too. You've become such a big part of my life. I've never met a man like you. You make my life perfect, too."

And then, as if all that weren't enough to tell him that she had totally misconstrued what he'd just said, she rose from her chair, rounded the kitchen table and dropped down into his lap. Then, circling her arms around his neck, she leaned forward and kissed him soundly on the mouth.

Yup, she was definitely under the wrong impression, he thought.

For a full nanosecond, Wheeler urged himself to correct the misunderstanding before things got out of hand. Or worse, before things got *in* hand. But just as he opened his mouth to do so, Audrey threaded her fingers through the hair at his nape and brushed her lips softly over his. And when she did, all rational thought just oozed right out of his brain. In its place there surged up inside him a need so strong, so profound, so inescapable, that it very nearly overwhelmed him. And at that point Wheeler could scarcely remember his own name, let alone any chivalric tendencies he may or may not have possessed.

Instinctively he roped his arms around her waist and pulled her closer, splaying his hands open over her back, thrusting his own fingers into the heavy dark silk of her hair. She gasped at the suddenness and enthusiasm of his response, and Wheeler took advantage of her reaction to taste her more deeply, more thoroughly. As his tongue found hers, she went limp against him, tilting her head first left, then right, in an effort to facilitate their joining.

He bunched a handful of her hair at her nape, cupping her head in his palm, turning her face so that he could plunder her mouth at will. She melted against him with an erotic sigh, curling her fingers into the fabric of his shirt, gripping it tightly, as if she never intended to let him go. Which was absolutely fine with Wheeler, because, at that moment, he fully intended to keep her in his lap for the rest of his natural life.

When he let his other hand drift lower, down to the taut curve of her fanny, she uttered a soft sigh of contentment, a sound that only deepened his need for her. Way back in the very corner of his brain, he thought he heard the whisper of a tiny, faint voice telling him this was a very bad idea. Then Audrey dipped her head to nuzzle the sensitive skin beneath his ear, sweeping a tentative hand across his chest and along his rib cage as she did so, and he forgot all about what the little voice had been trying to say.

She smelled incredible, he thought, growing intoxicated by her scent as he drew her nearer. A mixture of sweetness and spice, of purity and passion. And she felt... Oh, she felt so good. Soft and round and warm. Wheeler couldn't remember the last time he'd held a woman this close, couldn't recall ever needing one this desperately, couldn't say when he'd been as overcome with passion as he was at that moment.

Oh, wait, yes, he could. He had felt this way that last time in Audrey's apartment, when the two of them had come together in a sudden rush of hot demand. He'd felt then exactly the same way he did now—felt the same hunger, the same urgency, the same need. Only this time it was compounded. This time it roared up inside him like a tidal wave, silencing every warning bell, swamping every rational thought, carrying with it a fever pitch of desperation unlike anything he had ever felt before.

But where before they'd managed to curb their appetites, this time he wasn't altogether certain he'd be able to put a stop to things if they went too far. Which was just as well, he told himself. Because neither of them seemed to have any intention of stopping.

And even as he recognized the genesis of his response to her, even though he knew what he felt now was what he had felt then, what he had been feeling for months, Wheeler wasn't quite able—or willing—to put a name on those feelings. Not yet. Maybe not ever. In that moment, all he knew was that he wanted Audrey. He needed Audrey. He hungered for Audrey. And she clearly wanted and needed him, too.

So he stopped thinking and focused on his feelings. His needs. His desires. And all of those pointed toward her. He urged her closer, skimming the hand on her fanny down along her thigh, palming her soft flesh possessively before moving back up again. In response, she strummed her fingers slowly along his rib cage, then lower, over his flat belly, and briefly, daringly, along the buckle of his belt.

Okay, so much for the preliminaries, he thought. Time to get down to business.

Still cupping her fanny and thigh with one hand, Wheeler moved his other down along her shoulder before dipping inside the collar of her shirt. Her skin was like hot satin, sleek and smooth and soft, and he hesitated to see if she would object to his curious invasion. But Audrey only tunneled her fingers through his hair and raked her cheek against his temple, murmuring something that sounded like *Oh-yes-oh-yes-oh-yes-oh-yes*. Wheeler took it to be an encouraging response. So he tucked his fingers beneath the nearest button and expertly freed it from its loop.

He thought she gasped at his gesture, but the sound had been so soft, so breathy, he wondered if perhaps he had imagined it instead. Still feeling adventurous, he moved to the next button and deftly freed it, too. That in turn opened her shirt enough for him to see the whisper of purple silk beneath that hugged the plump curve of her breast. He swallowed hard, his mouth suddenly going dry. Then he dropped his fingers to the next button, unfastening it. Then he moved to the next, then the next and then the next.

At no point did Audrey discourage him. Instead she hugged him closer, wrapping her arms around his shoulders, skimming her hands down along his arms in a silent bid that urged Wheeler's fingers lower and lower and lower...

When he unfastened the final button, he hastily spread open her shirt, pushing it heedlessly over her shoulders, discarding it to the floor. Her ripe breasts strained against the confinement of her brassiere, spilling from the brief cups in invitation. Wheeler closed his hand over one of the lace-covered globes, cradling it, caressing it, claiming it.

Audrey uttered a whispery cry in response that sounded like both question and demand, urging Wheeler to continue. He tucked his fingers inside the soft silk, seeking the prize hidden at its center. Locating the dusky peak of her breast immediately, he rolled the taut pebble beneath his thumb, sinking his fingers into the ample curve of her bosom as he toyed delicately with her nipple.

"Oh," she whispered. "Oh, Wheeler."

He drove his hand further inside her brassiere, filling his

hand with her, palming her, playing with her, possessing her. Then, unable to deny himself the satisfaction of seeing her, he pushed the wisp of lace aside, grasping her breast in his hand. The ripe bud beckoned to him, and he dipped his head to close his mouth over her, drawing her as deeply inside him as he could, laving her with the flat of his tongue, teasing her with the tip.

Her fingers tightened in his hair, but instead of pushing him away, she tried to draw him closer still, mindless of the fact that they were already as intimately joined as they could be at that moment.

"Wheeler, please," she murmured on a gasp. "Oh, please. Oh, *please*..."

He honestly didn't know what she was asking him to do, whether she wanted him to stop or to step up his ministrations. He pulled back long enough to gaze at her face, and what he saw there tightened something fiercely inside him. Her lips were damp and lush, her eyes liquid fire, and her cheeks were stained by the tint of her arousal. And suddenly, more than anything, Wheeler wanted to be inside her. Deep. Hard. Fast. Forever.

Cradling her against him, he rose from the chair, lifting her effortlessly along for the ride. He fastened his mouth to hers and continued to kiss her as he crossed the short distance to where she slept at night. The house's turret encircled the bed like a loving embrace, and the last rays of the evening sun glowed golden behind the gauzy curtains covering the windows.

Gently he laid her at the center of the bed and followed her down, nestling between her legs, urging them apart as he joined her. She had taken his lead and gone to work on his buttons as they made their way across the apartment and had made short work of the garment. As she tried to push it from his shoulders, however, they both realized she had neglected one small detail—his necktie was still tied loosely around his open collar.

Laughing, Wheeler reached up to unknot it before one or both of them strangled him, but instead of untying it, he simply loosed it and looped it over his head, then tossed it, along with his shirt, to the floor.

Immediately Audrey splayed her hands open over his bare chest, burying her fingers in the rich, dark hair scattered along his entire torso. Flattening her palm, she pushed downward, slowly, slowly, slowly, until she encountered the waistband of his trousers. Fixing her gaze on his, she hesitated only a moment before unhooking his belt and tugging the length of leather free. Then she scooted his zipper down and, again after a small hesitation, she tucked her hand inside.

The feel of her fingers tripping along the rigid length of him, so gentle, so tentative, nearly pulled Wheeler apart at the seams. Gritting his teeth, he squeezed his eyes shut tight, an action Audrey must have interpreted as displeasure, because she immediately ceased her movements. So he rolled to his side, taking her with him. Circling her wrist with sure fingers, he pushed her hand back inside his trousers, closing his palm over the back of it. Then, with slow, measured movements, he rubbed both of their hands against himself, up and down, up and down, up…and…down.

The sensation was exquisite, sharp and heady. Audrey parted her lips slightly, and her eyes grew heavy and languid with desire. For long moments they only lay on their sides, their legs entwined, their hands united, caressing the long, rigid length of him. And when he didn't think he could tolerate any more without coming apart, Wheeler rolled their bodies again, until Audrey was atop him, straddling him.

Her brassiere had ceased to be functional some time ago, seeing as how both her breasts had spilled free of their confinement, and her hair was a wild tangle of curls that danced about her shoulders. She looked wanton and wonderful, sexy and sweet. And all he wanted in that moment was to stay there in her bed with her forever.

"Audrey," he managed in a ragged whisper. "I don't think it's going to surprise you, but suddenly, I want to make love to you. Very badly."

She nodded eagerly, breathlessly. "I want that, too."

"But I don't want you to do something you'll regret later," he hastened to add.

She smiled, her eyes going softer than before as she cupped a hand gently over his jaw. "Oh, Wheeler, I could never regret making love with you. Never."

He swallowed hard. There was something else he needed to tell her, he thought. But he couldn't quite remember now what it was. He opened his mouth to say *something*—he wasn't sure what—when Audrey touched two fingers to his lips.

"Don't," she said, her voice sounding urgent for some reason. "Don't tell me whatever it is you were going to tell me."

"But—"

"Don't," she repeated emphatically, the light seeming to fade from her eyes a bit. "You don't have to tell me how you feel. I *know* how you feel."

"But—"

"Just make love to me, Wheeler. Now."

He swallowed hard, telling himself it was foolish to do what they were about to do. But she was so beautiful, so soft. She felt so good. He wanted her so badly. And she clearly wanted him, too. Their desires were the same, their needs were identical.

She had just assured him that she knew how he felt about her, he reminded himself. She was an adult woman with some experience where the opposite sex was concerned. She knew what was what as well as he did. And she wanted the same thing that he did. If their reasons for wanting what they did were a bit off, well... Wheeler told himself they could work around it.

Even though he knew it wasn't love that had erupted between them—how could it be?—there was nevertheless something there that would link them forever. Fortune. Fate. Karma. Luck. Whatever it was, the link was infinite and unbreakable. There was no way he could resist what was happening.

So he stopped trying to.

"Shh," Audrey said, as if she concurred with the thoughts winding pell-mell through his head. She removed her fingers from his lips and quickly brushed her mouth over his. "Don't say anything more. I want this, Wheeler. I've wanted it for months." She smiled seductively. "I think I've wanted to get horizontal with you ever since that first day I walked into your office."

He couldn't help but smile in return. "You, too?" he asked. He'd heard women could be just as randy as men were, right out of the gate like that, but until now he'd never realized it was true. But he could see by the way Audrey was looking at him that she wanted him in exactly the same way he wanted her. Oh, boy.

Her smile changed then, transforming her entire face. He told himself it was only the warmth of the setting sun tumbling through the window that managed that glowing effect. Somehow, though, the light seemed to be coming from within her, not from without. He was astonished that she could be even more beautiful than he'd thought her before.

As he gazed upon her face, at the shimmering green of her eyes and the warm stain of pink on her cheeks, he still couldn't quite shake the feeling that there was something else they needed to talk about before they went any further, something else he needed to make clear. It was right there, hazy and indistinct, at the very back of his brain, but he couldn't quite make it come into focus. So he only contin-

ued to look longingly at Audrey, marveling again that he
was such a lucky man.

She straightened above him, reaching behind herself to
unhook her bra, tossing it to the floor without comment.
Then she stood long enough to wiggle out of her leggings
and panties, and returned to him naked, straddling him
again with a shy, secret little smile that was totally at odds
with the brazenness of her actions. He reached for her, running his palms over her bare thighs, up along the lush
curves of her hips and waist, filling each of his hands with
her ripe breasts, lifting them, palming them, squeezing
them. Then he scooted a hand behind her, over her bare
back, and urged her down so that he could have a taste of
her, too.

As if from a very great distance, the little voice at the
back of his head called out again, trying to make its presence known. But Audrey filled his mouth, his head, his
heart, until there was no room for anything more, and the
voice slowly drifted away unheard. After that, Wheeler surrendered to his senses and ceased to think at all.

Audrey couldn't imagine what had come over her to
make her behave in such a shameless, wanton way, but she
wasn't about to stop now. As Wheeler nuzzled her breasts
and flicked his tongue against her, as he sucked her deep
into his mouth, a wildfire erupted inside her, blazing a trail
to every cell in her body. Never before had a man wreaked
such havoc with her body, with her senses, with her sex-
uality. But this man...

This man, she thought, was the one. Wheeler Rush was
The One.

The one to make her feel graceful and beautiful. The one
who saw something in her no one else had seen. The one
who needed her. Who wanted her. Who desired her. The
one she would love forever.

The one who loved her back.

She marveled at that, still, the fact that Wheeler had

fallen in love with her. Because she was positive that was what he had been saying earlier, when he'd told her he needed her in his life to make it perfect. Sure, he hadn't come right out and said those three little words everyone longed to hear, but some people just had trouble putting voice to *I love you*. That didn't mean they didn't feel the emotion every bit as strongly as others did. Audrey was sure Wheeler had been telling her he loved her when he'd said what he had. What else could he have meant but that he loved her?

He *loved* her.

And she loved him. That was why she felt no inhibitions now, why she had no second thoughts for what she was doing. It was only natural that two people in love would turn to each other as she and Wheeler had tonight. And this was just the beginning, she thought. There would be more nights—and days—like this to come. Because she loved Wheeler. And Wheeler loved her. And that was how it would be forever.

Her thoughts evaporated when he rubbed his lips across her breasts, then moved his head lower, kissing her ribs, her belly, her navel. Somehow, she sensed her body moving forward, but she didn't realize what that meant until she felt Wheeler's lips skimming along the insides of her thighs. When she understood what was happening, she opened her eyes wide and tried to scoot backward. But he chuckled low and tightened his grip on her fanny, pushing her toward his mouth. She was about to voice an objection when he lifted his head and tasted her. Deeply. And then Audrey couldn't speak at all.

Over and over he creased her with his tongue, taunting her, teasing her, tantalizing her. The fingers on her buttocks dipped into the elegant line separating them, pushing her closer still to his marauding mouth. She rose up on her knees to escape the onslaught, but Wheeler followed, tumbling her onto her back when she tried to escape, burying his head between her legs with the clear intention of satisfying his appetites and hers. So Audrey lay limp on her bed with the sheets twined in her fingers, closed her eyes and enjoyed the ride.

She was very near sensual delirium when Wheeler finally moved away from her. For a moment all she could do was lie there insensate, wanting him, then gradually, somehow, she managed to open her eyes. She found him climbing back into bed naked, sheathed in a condom whose origin she didn't even want to contemplate right now. So she opened her arms to him, and Wheeler smiled, and then he was beside her again.

As she turned on her side to face him, he lifted her leg, bending it deeply, and settled it over his thigh. Then, as he covered her mouth with his and filled her with his tongue, he filled her lower, as well. He entered her as deeply as he could with that first thrust, propelling himself inside so thoroughly, so completely, that she cried out at the keenness of the union. Then he roped his arm across her back, withdrew some and drove himself inside again, to an even greater extent.

Instinctively Audrey arched against him, hurling her hips forward every time he plunged into her. Their rhythm was perfectly in sync; their bodies fit uniquely. Somehow, it occurred to her as she and Wheeler made love that, for the first time in her life, she felt fluid and graceful and elegant. She wasn't a klutz when she made love with him. She wasn't awkward. She wasn't unlucky. It only reaffirmed what she had already known—that love, true love, made everything different.

He rolled to his back then, moving Audrey astride him, and bucked hard against her, over and over and over again. With one final thrust, he arched against her and grew still, and a taut coil inside her that had been winding up tight let loose to expand in a riot of hot ripples that shook her to her very soul. For a moment they remained suspended as if time had ceased to exist. Then, slowly, Wheeler relaxed back onto the bed, bringing Audrey down with him.

He rolled their bodies once again until he lay atop her, then smoothed his hands over her hair and kissed her mouth. For a long time he kissed her, as if he needed to drink from her to revive himself. She linked her hands loosely at the small of his back and held him close, marveling again at what the two of them had found.

Eventually she found the strength to pull her head back from his. She gazed intently into his eyes, and very, very softly, she said, "I love you, Wheeler. I think I fell in love with you the day I walked into your office. And believe me when I tell you that that will never change. I'll always love you. Forever and ever."

He seemed to go rigid when she spoke. But she was too languid and mellow to analyze the gesture at the moment, so she put his reaction down to the aftermath of their loving and nothing more. Because Wheeler didn't say anything after that. He only gathered Audrey close, tangled his fingers in her hair, kissed her temple gently and stroked her bare body until she began to grow sleepy.

Tomorrow, she thought. They could talk about it tomorrow. As her conscious mind surrendered to the lethargy winding through her body, she smiled. Hey, after all, they'd have the rest of their lives together to talk.

When Audrey awoke in the morning, however, it was to discover that the rest of their lives together had been temporarily interrupted, by, of all things, Wheeler's sudden and complete disappearance from it.

Although she had forgotten to set the alarm clock the night before—she *had* sort of had other things on her mind when she went to bed—she still managed to wake up at seven, right on schedule. Which was totally unlike her, because even when she set the alarm, something usually went wrong and she wound up oversleeping. Then she would hurt herself while she rushed around to get ready, and then she would end up being late for whatever she had scheduled, and then…

Well, that wasn't important right now. What was important was the fact that she had woken up alone after a night of deliriously satisfying lovemaking. Well, alone save the two cats sleeping in their usual place on the wide window ledge, she amended. The two cats who were eyeing her with identical gleams of speculation in their eyes, she noted further with a frown.

She stuck out her tongue at them and went about reassessing her situation. Because in waking up alone, all the certainty Audrey had felt the night before, about how good things were between her and Wheeler and where they were going in the infinite future that lay spread out before them, evaporated in a puff of fond memories.

She pushed her hair out of her eyes and sat up, only to discover that she ached in places she hadn't realized could ache. Funny, how such different muscles got used when a person was making wild, jungle love. Then she nudged that thought aside, too, and tried to find some evidence that Wheeler Rush had in fact been in her apartment the night before, doing all those delicious things to her that he had done. More than once, if memory served.

But there was nothing to suggest he had been present anywhere but in her dreams, nary a stray sock or scent of a man to be found. The pillow opposite her was rumpled and crushed, so, clearly, she had shared her bed with *some*one. Nevertheless, with the way things were, that someone could have been anyone.

But it *had* been Wheeler, she recalled. He *had* been there. And he *had* made sweet, wondrous, exquisite love to her. Of that much, if nothing else, Audrey was absolutely positive. But now he was gone, and with him, any certainty she might have entertained that the two of them had been under the influence of the same aphrodisiac last night—namely love.

Call her an alarmist, but a man who had just discovered he was wildly in love with his secretary didn't take a powder the morning after making love to her, even if his business was on shaky ground and he had to get to work early. The least Wheeler could have done was wake her long enough to tell her goodbye. Then again, it would also have been nice if he had seen fit to give her a lift so she didn't have to take the bus. Granted, he liked to be in the office much earlier than she needed to be, which was why he had never driven her in before, but hey...

When you woke up in the same bed together, a ride to work just seemed the logical next step in the relationship, never mind admitting you loved each other and couldn't survive without each other and wanted to spend the rest of your lives together.

But surely Wheeler felt the same way she did, Audrey tried to reassure herself, crossing her arms over her breasts in a gesture that felt way too much like self-preservation. He must feel the same way she did. As she rose naked from her bed and snatched her robe from the chair where it perpetually lay, she told herself, too, that no one—no one—could have made love to her the way Wheeler had last night unless he loved her.

But as she went about her usual morning routine, readying herself for work, Audrey began to feel less and less certain about Wheeler's feelings for her, even as she grew more and more assured about what she felt for him. She loved him. It was that simple. She had loved him probably since that first day at work. And she would do whatever was necessary to preserve the fragile relationship the two of them had discovered together.

Quickly she made herself some cinnamon-raisin toast—without setting off the smoke alarm once—and consumed it with her morning coffee—without spilling so much as a crumb or a drop on her robe. She dressed in a form-fitting ivory sheath—without tearing the fabric or losing a button—and donned a pair of matching ivory stockings—without snagging the delicate silk. Then she carefully applied her makeup—without once poking herself in the eye with the mascara wand or accidentally dragging her lipstick across her chin—and arranged her hair atop her head—without having to fight one snarl. Then she gathered up her things—which were all right where they were supposed to be and not hiding under a chair or the bed—and headed out the front door.

And as she made her way toward the bus stop on Bardstown Road, it occurred vaguely to Audrey that for the first time in her entire life, she'd survived her usual morning ritual without one, single, solitary thing going wrong. It could only be a good sign, she thought. Couldn't it?

Nine

As he sat in his office feeling bemused, bothered and befuddled, Wheeler slowly replayed in his head every moment that had passed the night before. He could still scarcely believe that he and Audrey Finnegan—*Audrey Finnegan*—had done what they had done.

He could scarcely believe that the two of them had come together in that wild frenzy of lovemaking that had lasted most of the night. He could scarcely believe that one minute they'd been discussing business-as-usual stuff and the next he'd been inhaling great gulps of her sweet-smelling skin. And he could scarcely believe he had left this morning in a panic without even telling her goodbye.

He still felt guilty about that. And he still felt dogged by the odd sensation he'd had last night that there was something very important he'd needed to tell Audrey before the two of them had taken that final and irrevocable step toward intimacy. More than anything else right now, he wanted to remember what that something was. As he tried to recall, he dissected the evening bit by bit, breath by breath, action by action, to figure out exactly where and how he'd gone wrong.

First, they had shared a meal together—nothing major in that. He'd shared meals with lots of women, lots of times, Audrey Finnegan included. So that part of the scenario didn't bother him at all. After dinner they'd cleaned up the kitchen together and enjoyed a cup of coffee—again, nothing worthy of note there, except maybe for the remarkably bad way that Audrey made coffee. Then, at some point during coffee, he'd told her how important she'd become to him, and then she'd kissed him, and then he'd unbuttoned her shirt.

Okay, so maybe this was where things had moved onto shaky ground, he thought, his body heating up at where his memories were taking him. Because after all that, of course, the two of them had found their way to her bed and had proceeded to do all those incredibly erotic, explicit things together. Wheeler let his mind rove freely over that for a few minutes before continuing, closing his eyes as he ruminated over the scents and sounds and sights of Audrey burrowing naked against him.

Hoo-kay, he thought, forcing his eyes open and his brain back on track. Enough of that. No need to drive himself to distraction when there was work to be done and errors to be remembered. He shifted in his chair to alleviate the sudden tightness that seemed to have overtaken his entire body as his recollections had grown more graphic. Ahem. Now then. So…after they'd enjoyed that slow, thorough exploration of each other's bodies and libidos, he thought, what had happened next was…

Audrey had told him she loved him.

Oh, yeah. Now he remembered. It dawned on Wheeler then, like a sledgehammer upside the head, what it was he had wanted to tell her the night before. As they'd been gathering steam and approaching that point of no return, he had meant to make clear to her that although whatever happened between the two of them sexually would be many things—passionate, wondrous, mind-bending, incandescent—it wouldn't be love. Not on his part, at any rate. He needed Audrey, yes, in a variety of ways. But love? No, no, no, no, no. That was *much* too dangerous, where she was concerned.

How could he have forgotten to point that out to her? How could he have omitted that one small detail? And what was he going to do about it now?

No sooner had the questions erupted in his head than there came a trio of quick, quiet raps at his office door. Only Audrey knocked with such a soft, undemanding touch, and for a single, delirious moment, he wondered if he had time to hurl himself out the window behind his desk. Not that the fall would kill him and save him from this unavoidable confrontation—seeing as how he was on the first floor of the building, he probably wouldn't even maim himself—but it might buy him a little time if he escaped for the day.

"Wheeler? Can we talk?"

So much for escape. Her voice coming through the door was tentative, uncertain, wary. Something inside him tightened fiercely when he heard her say his name the way she had. Before, whenever Audrey had addressed him, there had been a breezy, carefree kind of happiness to the sound. She had always smiled when she spoke his name, and her eyes had always been lit with a kind of fond affection. Now, however, he could tell without even seeing her that she almost certainly wasn't smiling.

"Come on in, Audrey," he said halfheartedly, steeling himself for the inevitable.

At this point, however, he honestly didn't know what to say. Probably because he honestly didn't know what to think. And that was doubtless because he honestly didn't know how he felt.

She pushed the door open slowly, gingerly, then passed through and closed it behind her with a quiet *click*. For a moment she simply leaned back against it, her gaze skittering about the room as if she wanted to look at him, but just didn't quite know how to manage it. Then, clearly having made up her mind about something, she pushed herself away from the door and took a step toward him.

Wheeler opened his mouth to offer his customary caution about the rug, because she invariably tripped over the edge of it when she entered his office, hurtling her body forward. But before he could utter the warning aloud, she stepped easily, almost gracefully, over the rug's edge *and* a little bump beyond it, without even seeming to notice either was there. It was the first time in Wheeler's memory that Audrey had made an entrance into his office without, well...making an entrance.

Even as she approached him, she still didn't look at him, and instead focused her gaze on some point on the wall above his head. Not sure why he did it—hey, he was every bit as willing to avoid eye contact as she was—Wheeler rose, putting his face at her eye level. When he did, she shot her attention to the left, gazing at something there instead.

He moved around to the front of his desk, then hoisted himself atop it, his legs dangling before him, his fingers hooked loosely together in his lap. There was a time when he thought the posture made him look casual and nonchalant. Now, however, he wondered if it just didn't make him look tense and anxious instead. Because suddenly, that was exactly how he felt.

"When I woke up this morning," she said softly, swallowing hard, still not looking at him, "you, um...you were gone."

He nodded, wishing he could come up with something to say that wouldn't sound cold, careless or clichéd. But all that came out was a very quiet "Yes." He wanted to say

more, knew she deserved an explanation. But seeing as how
he had no idea what might explain the miasma of doubts
and concerns swirling through his brain, he remained silent.

She continued to study the wall behind him and added,
"I was...I was all alone."

"Yes," he said again, still struggling to find some excuse
that might make sense of his actions. But none was forth-
coming. All he could manage was a lamely offered "I'm
sorry."

She nodded and swallowed hard again, but still she
didn't look at him. "It made me wonder...you know..."

She inhaled deeply, then finally, finally turned her head
to look at him. For one brief moment, her eyes locked with
his, and what he saw in them nearly stopped his heart. A
deep and profound sadness unlike anything he had ever
encountered from Audrey before. No matter how bad things
had gotten in his business, no matter how unfortunate, how
clumsy, how embarrassing their encounters had been, she
had never been anything but upbeat and positive. Now,
however, for the first time, she seemed to be overcome by
a genuine, heartfelt melancholy. And he knew it was because of what he'd done.

For several moments she only studied his face in silence.
Then, evidently losing her nerve, she let her gaze skitter
away again. "It, um, it made me wonder," she tried again,
"why you left that way. Without even saying goodbye, I
mean."

That makes two of us, he thought.

When he'd first awakened just before dawn that morning,
Wheeler had been a bit disoriented. Not just because he
didn't recognize his surroundings, but because he didn't
recognize his feelings, either. It had taken him only a few
seconds to realize he was in Audrey's bed, with Audrey
sleeping peacefully beside him, her warm, fragrant body
curled into his with much familiarity and affection. What
he *hadn't* understood was why the discovery of her sleeping

beside him that way, along with the memories of all they had shared the night before, felt, for a moment, so good and so right.

It had made no sense. He'd never much been one for morning afters. That was why he'd never spent the entire night with a woman. He'd always made sure he was gone long before the sun came up, making a clean break and a thorough retreat to *his* place, to *his* stuff. Wheeler liked living alone. He liked the solitude, the quiet, the peace. He liked knowing where everything was, and the fact that everything stayed in its place. He just liked things neat and tidy and ordered.

At least, that was how he *used* to like things. Suddenly, however...

He sighed heavily. Upon waking this morning, he'd realized immediately that neat and tidy and ordered had just flown right out the window. But that wasn't what had bothered him. What had bothered him was that he hadn't *cared* that those things had gone out the window. He hadn't *cared* that his life had just blown up in his face. He hadn't *cared* that he had just linked himself in the most basic, most intimate way imaginable with the most unfortunate woman alive. All he'd *cared* about was making love to Audrey again.

And that, he'd decided pretty quickly, was something he definitely needed to think about before he made another move.

But even after thinking about it all morning, he was no closer to a resolution now than he had been hours ago. He studied Audrey as she waited for an answer to her question. Her green eyes held concern, and she nibbled her lip—that ripe, luscious, red lip—with anxiety. She had shifted her weight to one foot, and the lush curve of her hip drew his eye.

She was a beautiful, gentle, sweet woman, he reminded himself, even if she was unbelievably unfortunate. She deserved a lover who wouldn't abandon her under a cover of darkness the way he had. She deserved a man who had some idea of what it was he felt for her. She deserved a man whose primary reason for wanting her in his life extended beyond her value as a good-luck charm. She deserved better than Wheeler.

Didn't she?

"So why did you?" she asked when he still didn't answer, scattering his thoughts, rattling his emotions. "Leave, I mean? Without waking me up first and telling me you were going?"

He had no idea how to answer her question. So he said the only thing he knew to say. "I don't know," he told her honestly. "I don't know why I left this morning the way I did. I just..."

"What?"

He inhaled deeply and released the breath in a slow, ragged stream of air. "Audrey," he said, adopting his most serious, no-nonsense, I'm-the-boss voice. "Sit down."

She hesitated only a moment before doing as he'd instructed, seating herself in the chair opposite him, perched on the edge as if ready for flight should their discussion become too much to tolerate. She crossed one leg over the other, and it occurred to him that she somehow seemed more graceful today than she had been in the past. He scanned her person for signs of injury, the ubiquitous Band-Aid that always seemed to decorate some part of her anatomy. But today, there was none. Today, she seemed more confident of herself, more poised, and much less the receptacle for ill fortune.

He sighed heavily, telling himself to just be honest and correct the misconception that had led them to this point. There was no sense in perpetuating a lie, even if being truthful now would doubtless jeopardize the tenuous nature of their newly changed relationship. Because in spite of how much he had enjoyed the intimacy they had shared the night before, there was no point in pursuing it, he told himself. There was no future in any affair the two of them might have. To let Audrey think otherwise would simply make things worse than they already were.

Sure, once he made that clear to her, there would be some awkwardness and discomfort between them for a while, until they smoothed over the rough spots. But in the long run it would be best if each knew where the other stood. Eventually, he was certain, they could go back to being professional. Back to business as usual. It was, Wheeler assured himself, for the best.

"Last night," he began slowly, "after dinner, when I told you how important you'd become to me?"

He turned the words up at the end, making the statement into a question instead. In response, Audrey nodded slowly, and he thought she looked a little happier than she had before. A lump of something hard and icy settled in his stomach when he realized he was about to squash whatever optimism might be budding in her brain.

"Well, when I said that," he began again, "I don't think you understood it the way I meant it."

Two bright spots of pink appeared on her cheeks, and her lips parted fractionally, as if she wanted to say something but had no idea what. Wheeler sympathized; he felt pretty much the same way. In spite of that, he pressed on.

"When I said that my life fell apart while you were gone, but that everything was right again, now that I had you back, it didn't mean what you thought it meant."

"Then tell me what it did mean." Her voice came out soft and shallow, and very, very scared.

He sighed again, tightening his fingers together before him. "I didn't mean… It wasn't… I didn't… What I meant was…"

"What?" she demanded, the word scarcely audible.

He looked at her straight on and forced the statement out

of his mouth. "I didn't say that because I'd fallen in love with you, Audrey."

She closed her eyes at his roughly offered statement, as if she didn't want to look at him when he said whatever else he had to say. "Then what did you mean?" she asked softly again.

This wasn't going at all the way Wheeler had planned. Feeling restless and sick to his stomach, he pushed himself away from the desk and paced to the far side of the room. "Audrey," he said as he went, forcing a steadiness into his voice that he was nowhere close to feeling. "We really do need to talk about this. And it's not going to be easy."

Audrey snapped her eyes open at Wheeler's announcement, wishing that by doing so, she would awaken from what she hoped was just a very bad dream. Unfortunately, when she opened her eyes, she found that she was indeed seated in his office, that he was indeed pacing restlessly about the room as if he couldn't stand being any closer to her than he had to be, and that she was indeed listening to him tell her that she had totally misunderstood what she had thought was his declaration of love for her the night before.

Oh, God, she thought as a wave of nausea rolled over in her belly. Could this possibly get any worse?

She swallowed hard, her body going rigid at the knowledge that yes, it could definitely get worse, and would doubtless do just that any minute now. Every time a man had told her they needed to talk about something, it had always meant that *he* needed to talk and *she* needed to listen. And every time, what he'd had to say was invariably something she didn't want to hear.

In spite of that, she said, "I thought that's what we were doing. Talking, I mean."

She sensed, more than saw Wheeler turn and begin pacing the other way. But she kept her back to him, because she honestly didn't want to look at him when he told her how much he didn't love her. She could already hear what he was going to say. That making love and being in love were two totally different things where he was concerned, and he'd thought he'd made that clear. She should know the song by heart by now, she told herself. She'd heard it often enough in her life.

She could practically recite the words along with him as he paced behind her and said, "Although I certainly *care* for you, Audrey…"

Uh-oh. That was the kiss of death, as far as she was concerned. A man only told a woman he cared about her when he didn't really care about her at all.

"And although you're *vitally important* to me…"

Ooo, that was even worse than being cared for.

"And although I can't *possibly manage* without you…"

That did it. The minute he finished his little speech, she was resigning. There was no way she was going to hang around being vitally important to someone who cared about her and couldn't possibly manage without her. Uh-uh. No way. No how. A girl had to hold on to some scrap of her dignity, after all.

She decided then and there that she would give him her two weeks' notice on her way out today—even with the way things were between them, she didn't have it in her to leave him in the lurch. But after that she would be little more than a footnote in the Wheeler Rush story.

He ceased his pacing then and moved to stand beside her. Audrey kept her eyes fixed firmly forward and refused to look at him, bracing herself for what she knew was coming next.

"I don't love you, Audrey," he said.

Wow. It hurt even worse than she'd thought it would, the words piercing her down to her very soul. She squeezed her eyes shut tight in an effort to keep at bay the tears she felt threatening. But he didn't seem to notice, because he went right on talking, oblivious to her pain.

"I'm sorry," he said. "But I don't. I can't. It's just not in me right now to manage a romantic relationship with a woman. Any woman. I have my business to see to, and there are just too many uncertainties in my life right now, and I can't contribute to those uncertainties by pursuing a relationship that may or may not work out, and please try to understand."

She nodded slowly, thinking that he sounded as if he were on the verge of babbling incoherently. Maybe he wasn't as cool about this as he seemed to be. Then again, did that really matter? He was saying he didn't feel for her the way she felt for him, and that he had no intention of even exploring their relationship to see where it might lead. He was bailing out. He didn't love her. That was all that mattered to Audrey.

She stood, still averting her gaze from his. "I see. Well. That's that then, isn't it? I guess that pretty much defines the difference between you and me, doesn't it?"

He hesitated for a moment before asking, "What do you mean?"

She turned to study him full on. "I mean that whatever is—was—happening between you and me, I didn't consider it an uncertainty. I thought it was a sure thing."

His eyes, his entire face, seemed to soften some at that, and he lifted a hand toward her. "Audrey..."

She jerked her head back and took two steps in retreat before he could touch her, amazed that his expression grew pained when she did. "But it's good you made your feelings clear, Wheeler," she told him, surprised at the energy with which she delivered the statement. She sure didn't feel energetic at the moment. "Not every man would tell the truth in a situation like this. A lot of guys would just go on taking advantage of a woman who loved them, for as long as they could. I guess I should be grateful that you're an honest guy."

Ha. Grateful. That was a laugh.

"Audrey, please..." He expelled a restless sound and shoved a big hand brutally through his hair. "I could never—"

"I better go," she interrupted him, unwilling to hear anything else he might have to say. She smoothed her hands down over her dress when what she really wanted to do was hit something. Hard. Through no small effort, she somehow willed her tears not to fall. "I have work to do. Thanks for setting the record straight and everything. Thanks for clearing up all that confusion for me. I'll just, um..."

Her bravado deserted her then, causing her voice to break on the last few words, making it impossible for her to finish any mindless little platitude she'd been about to utter. Which was just as well, she decided, because she probably would have ended up blathering like an idiot. With as much dignity as she could muster, she spun on her heel and headed for the door, swiping her palms under her eyes as she went.

"Audrey, wait," Wheeler called from behind.

Yeah, right, she thought. The last thing she wanted to do was wait around and let him watch her fall apart piece by piece. She gripped the doorknob firmly and began to twist it to the right, but his hand over hers stopped the motion before she could complete it. She felt his body behind hers from her heels to her head, and she inhaled deeply of his scent and his warmth, because she knew she might not ever have this opportunity again. But all that did was make her feel even more miserable, more melancholy, more bereft.

"Don't leave like this," he said softly. "Please."

"Leave like what?" she asked, striving for flippancy, knowing she only sounded foolish instead. "Like a woman who's just humiliated herself beyond repair? Hey, don't worry about me. I've survived worse episodes than this. You forget—I'm the unluckiest woman alive, remember? Jinxed to the max. Hexed to the very limit."

"That's not true," he said. "You're the best good-luck charm I've ever had."

Something about the way he said that halted anything else Audrey might have said herself. She released the doorknob and spun around to face him, studying him through narrowed eyes. He was still much too close for comfort, but she didn't try to move away. "What do you mean by that?" she asked, suspicion mixed with fear congealing in the pit of her stomach.

He seemed to realize then that he probably shouldn't have said what he'd just said. His eyes widened fearfully, and his cheeks were stained by the tint of embarrassment. But the words were out, hanging between them like a load of dirty laundry, and Audrey wasn't about to let it go until she had a satisfactory answer.

"Wheeler?" she spurred him. "What did you mean by that? What did you mean when you said I was your good-luck charm?"

But he said nothing in response, only set his jaw firmly and shifted his gaze from hers, as if he couldn't quite meet her eyes.

"You hired me back because you thought I brought you good luck?" she asked. "Not because you missed me or thought I did a good job, but because I brought you good luck? Is that what all this has been about? Is that what you meant last night after dinner?"

In response he only dropped his gaze to the floor and said nothing.

She shook her head slowly as understanding dawned. "That was what you meant when you said having me back made everything perfect, wasn't it? It was perfect again, but not because you loved me. Because you thought I brought you good luck." She chuckled once, but there was no joy in the sound. "That's it, isn't it?" she asked. "You really think I'm a good-luck charm. You never cared about me as a person at all. I'm right, aren't I?"

But instead of replying, he only continued to stare down at the floor.

"Answer me," she demanded softly.

He looked up again, his expression miserable as he met her gaze. "It's not like you think," he said.

Somehow she managed to keep her voice level when she said, "Then make me think otherwise."

He growled fretfully, raking both hands through his hair before spinning on his heel and retreating to his desk. "It all revolved around you," he said as he went. "The day you arrived in my office, things started turning around for me. The business started to recover, I started getting good ideas again, I landed new clients." He turned again, leaning back against his desk, shoving his hands deep into his trouser pockets. "At first I didn't think that much about it. I just thought my downturn had finally reversed, you know?"

Audrey nodded slowly, crossing her arms over her midsection. "Go on."

"Then, when it came time to hire Rosalie back—you were, after all, only temporary, Audrey—"

"In more ways than one, evidently," she interjected.

In response to her comment, he frowned. "It wasn't like that," he insisted.

"Then tell me what it *was* like."

He eyed her intently before continuing. "After I let you go, within days the business started to fail again. Clients were in an uproar, my staff was sniping at each other, my creativity was shot... Nothing was getting done except that we were losing what ground we'd gained. And the more I thought about it, the more I realized that you were the key. When you worked for me, everything went great. When you didn't work for me, everything went to hell. You brought me good luck, Audrey. Deny it all you want, but it's true. So I found you and hired you back."

"Because you thought I'd turn the business back around," she finished for him.

"Yes," he told her contritely.

"Because you think I'm your good-luck charm."

"Yes."

Audrey could hardly believe her ears. But it all made sense now. So this was why he had continued to employ her, even though she was clearly not cut out for secretarial work. All this time she'd been thinking that Wheeler had hired her back and kept her on because he cared deeply for her and couldn't stand the thought of losing her.

Well, of course, she realized now, he *couldn't* stand the thought of losing her. Not because he cared deeply for her. But because he thought she brought him good luck.

Oh, now *that* was a good one. Audrey Finnegan, jinxed to the max, hexed to the limit, bringing good luck to someone else. Well, hardy-har-har-har. She hoped the gods were having a good laugh at her expense. Because she sure didn't find any humor in the situation herself.

She stared at him in silence for a long time, then dropped her hands back to her sides and slowly shook her head. "Wheeler, you're an idiot, you know that?"

He arched his eyebrows in surprise. Of all the things she could have said, that clearly wasn't what he'd expected. "I beg your pardon?"

"I said, 'You're an idiot,'" she repeated, more forcefully this time. For emphasis, she fisted her hands on her hips and glared at him.

He gaped at her. "Why would say something like that?"

"Because it's true," she insisted. "You're an idiot."

He pushed himself away from the desk and crossed the room until he stood immediately in front of her. "Well, you don't have to keep saying it over and over like that."

His nearness and righteous indignation caused some of her conviction to waver, but she held her ground, pushing herself up on tiptoe to get in his face. "Yeah, well... I wanted to make sure you heard me when I told you you're an idiot."

He frowned harder. "I heard you."

"Good."

He eased off some then. "I just don't know what the hell you meant."

Somehow Audrey refrained from flattening her palm and smacking him on the forehead. Hard. "I mean, you'd rather think I'm a good-luck charm than to accept what's really happening between the two of us. You're too stupid to see the obvious."

He narrowed his eyes at her. "I am *not* stupid."

"You are if you've been thinking that things turned around for you because I'm your good-luck charm."

His lips parted fractionally in clear confusion. "Audrey, what are you talking about?"

She shook her head at him again, but didn't even try to explain. If he was too shortsighted to see what was as plain as the nose on his face, then she certainly wasn't going to try to lead him around by that nose. She wasn't going to be the one who told him that the reason things had turned around in his business was *not* because she'd brought him good luck, but because she'd brought him something else entirely different, something infinitely more important.

Wheeler was going to have to figure it out for himself, or he would never understand what had happened. He would never realize that there were some things in life that were far more potent than tokens of chance. He'd spend the rest of his life believing in good-luck charms, and he'd never have faith in himself. Or in her. Or in the thing that had really brought them together.

Sometimes a woman just had to know when to surrender, when to retreat, when to regroup, she thought. And this was one of those times. She'd done what she could. The rest was up to Wheeler. Hey, he was a smart guy. Usually. Eventually he'd figure it out.

She hoped.

Without a word she strode over to his worktable and tore

a sheet of graph paper from the pad that lay benignly in the wire basket hanging beneath. Then she rooted through his pencil box until she found something normal to write with. And then, in tidy little letters upon the neat blue boxes, she wrote the date, followed by the words, "I resign, effective immediately. Yours sincerely, Audrey Finnegan." She signed off with a flourish, then crossed to Wheeler again and held the paper up for him to see.

Quickly he scanned the words thereon, and immediately the color drained from his face. When his gaze met hers again, his eyes were wide with panic.

"I was going to give you two weeks' notice," she said, "but all things considered, I think it would be best to conclude this as quickly as possible. So I'm quitting now."

"*Quitting?*" he echoed, the word erupting in shock. "You can't quit. Audrey..." He was pleading with her now. "You can't quit. You can't."

"I can, too," she told him. "Watch me."

"No!" He shouted the word so loudly, she flinched. He lifted a hand toward her, then dropped it back to his side without touching her. His voice was much softer when he added, "You can't go. You can't abandon me this way."

This time she was the one to gape at Wheeler. "Why not?" she countered. "You abandoned me."

"What?" he said, obviously confused. "I never abandoned you."

"You abandoned me the minute you started seeing me as a good-luck charm," she told him. "I'm *not* a good-luck charm, Wheeler. To you or anybody. And if that's the only reason you hired me back, if that's the only reason you wanted me in your life, I'd rather go back to washing dogs. At least they have genuine feelings for me. They don't keep me around because they think I've sealed their fate."

"But you can't leave me," he petitioned softly. "You can't. Audrey..." He expelled a helpless sound, and his entire body slumped forward in defeat. "If you go, I'll lose everything."

Her heart hammered hard at that. "Wheeler, you've already lost everything," she said softly before turning toward the door again. "It's up to you now, whether or not you get it back."

"But—"

"But nothing. Yeah, maybe I helped you get things back on track in your life. But *not* because I'm your good-luck charm. Think about it. I'll be around."

"But—"

She tugged the door open and passed through it, turning one last time to look at him as she left. "Goodbye," she said softly. "If you figure it out, give me a call. Otherwise, don't ever bother me again."

Ten

Surprisingly, in the few weeks that followed Audrey's departure, very little changed in the running of Wheeler's office. In the running of his personal life, however...

Well, there *was* the small matter of that great, gaping hole inside him that chilled him to his core, a vast and vacant emptiness that seemed to stretch on to a bleak and black eternity, a dark and dangerous chasm he couldn't seem to fill no matter how hard he tried, an infinite and icy void that nothing, absolutely nothing, could warm, leaving him to feel a desperate and desolate loneliness unlike anything he had ever experienced before in his entire life.

Oh, but hey, other than that, everything was just peachy.

Audrey's absence in the office had been a relatively simple matter to remedy. Although he'd been tempted to call One-Day-at-a-Timers again—to hire a temp until he could figure out what the hell he had to do to get Audrey back—Wheeler wound up trying another agency instead. One-Day-at-a-Timers was simply too big a reminder of what he'd found and lost in Audrey. But the other service had sent a secretary who was perfectly capable of taking on the task of managing the offices of Rush Commercial Designs, Inc. For the time being.

At least until he could figure out what the hell he had to do to get Audrey back.

The temp's name was Melinda, and she was a far, far cry from Audrey. She didn't have Audrey's questionable poise, or Audrey's dubious fashion sense, or Audrey's even more dubious flair for office machinery. Melinda never blew anything up, never set off the smoke alarm when she made microwave popcorn, never crashed the computer system right when Wheeler needed it for something very important. Melinda never had a problem with the way the phone worked, never cut off a client when she was transferring a call. She never tripped over the rug, never had to tug her clothes back into place after some embarrassing mishap—mainly because her clothes were very sensible, and she never *had* any embarrassing mishaps. And God knew her coffee was *nothing* like Audrey's.

But she didn't have Audrey's smile, either. Or Audrey's laughter. Or Audrey's unique way of looking at things. Or Audrey's dangerous curves and soft shoulders, for that matter. As efficient and reliable as Melinda was, she wasn't...well, she wasn't Audrey.

And Wheeler found that he really, really resented all of Melinda's efficiency. He really, really hated the way she handled crises smoothly and ran things perfectly. He was really, really bothered by her keen of duty and responsibility and her knack for getting everything done on time and in order. It just didn't feel right, having her as a part of the Rush Commercial Designs, Inc. team.

His clients noticed that, too, he realized immediately, because every time he picked up his extension to take a phone call, the first words out of the client's mouth were, invariably, ''Where the hell is Audrey?'' Then Wheeler would always have to explain that she had quit. And then he'd always have to sit through a litany from the client about how if he'd been a better boss and taken better care of her, she never would have left. That was inescapably followed by the client's curiosity about whether she'd gone to another commercial design firm, and if so, could Wheeler please offer a referral?

That, of course, would lead him to tell the truth, that no, he didn't know where Audrey was working now, but he was pretty sure she'd left the secretarial profession for good, and could they please just discuss the business matter at hand? Please? Grudgingly the client would relent and get to the point of the phone call, and business would continue on as usual.

So all in all, nothing much had changed around the office. But all in all, things just weren't the same around the office.

They weren't the same outside the office, either. With Audrey's departure, Wheeler found that his entire life felt empty. His apartment seemed quieter somehow, even though she'd never once visited him there. The office seemed more sterile somehow, less warm, less inviting, even though nothing had materially changed. His drives home from work were equally lonely, because he no longer had the happy chatter of Audrey to keep him company. When he ate his meals alone, an activity that had never bothered him before, he suddenly felt uncomfortable in his solitude. And at night, as he strove for sweet slumber, he found himself instead beset by memories of making love to Audrey.

But even more than the sensual experiences the two of them had shared, Wheeler found himself missing the simple day-to-day interaction. Whenever his office door opened, he steeled himself for one of Audrey's spectacular spills...only to have Melinda enter gracefully with some annoying business detail. Whenever he exited his office, he prepared himself for whatever crisis of machinery Audrey might be battling, hoping he would survive it without one or both of them being electrocuted...only to find Melinda seated poised at her station, typing effortlessly away on her keyboard.

Why hadn't his business fallen apart with Audrey's departure? he wondered one sunny, hot, Friday afternoon in August, as he collected his things to go home. He'd been so certain she was integral to the well-being of his business because she brought him good luck. It only made sense that without her, everything would fall apart again. But it hadn't. Why?

Aside from the brief grumblings of his clients about her sudden absence, there was really nothing much changed at Rush Commercial Designs, Inc. Wheeler was still coming up with good ideas, and no one was threatening to take their business elsewhere. Granted, he hadn't landed many new clients—or even one, for that matter—but that was to be expected. A business could only grow so far, so fast. It was only natural that things would level off. Certainly there was nothing catastrophic about the leveling. Professionally, everything was sound.

Obviously Audrey *hadn't* been essential in maintaining his prosperity, he realized as he snapped his briefcase shut and crossed toward the office door. He halted mid-stride as he finally forced himself to make that confession. Audrey hadn't brought him good luck, he repeated silently to himself. She hadn't been his good-luck charm.

At least, not in any professional capacity.

Of course, things *had* gone to hell in his personal life with her departure, he realized further. He was lonely and bored and short-tempered without her. But that wasn't really because he'd suffered any kind of downturn in his usual good luck.

Was it?

If he had her back, he thought further, then he wouldn't

feel so alone. Of course, his loneliness wouldn't be assuaged because she brought him good luck.

Would it?

Still puzzling over that, he forced his legs to move forward again, knowing what he would find when he exited his office into the reception area beyond—emptiness, that's what he would find. Melinda and the rest of his staff were long gone by now, because only Wheeler stayed past the dinner hour. He told himself that was just because he was a conscientious worker, and *not* because he simply didn't want to go home to an empty apartment and a lonely dinner table.

That naturally led him to start thinking about Audrey again. And as a result, as he passed through his office door, he halfway expected to see her seated at her old desk— he'd never quite been able to call it Melinda's desk—hunting and pecking in that two-fingered way she had of typing. He could almost smell the aroma of burned wiring, could almost conjure the bitter flavor of her coffee on his tongue. If he closed his eyes, he thought, he could even recall those little sounds of frustration and annoyance she'd always muttered at the computer.

But Audrey wasn't there when he passed through his door. Nobody was. The office was, as he'd expected it to be, empty. Just like the rest of his life.

He shouldn't have taken Audrey for granted, he thought. Then he tried to tell himself that he *hadn't* taken her for granted. How could he have? She'd been his good-luck charm, for God's sake, the one thing in his life that made everything right. No way would he take something like that for granted.

He started toward the front door, then stopped suddenly to replay his thoughts. "Something like that," he repeated to himself. Some*thing* like *that*. Audrey wasn't a *thing*, he reminded himself. She wasn't a *that*. She was a person. A human being. Maybe he should have remembered that, in-

stead of focusing on her status and value as a potential
magic talisman to keep the wolves at bay.

Maybe he should have realized a long time ago that she
wasn't a magic talisman. She was infinitely more than that,
had brought considerably more to his life than a good-luck
charm could bring. Audrey wasn't a good-luck charm, he
repeated to himself. She was a woman. A woman who
loved him.

A woman who maybe he loved back?

The question erupted in his brain with all the force of an
atomic warhead, and he found himself staggering backward. Good heavens. Was that what all this had really been
about? Could that be what Audrey had been talking about
the day she'd resigned? Was it love, not luck, that she had
brought to his life? Love, not luck, that had made all the
difference? Love, not luck, that had made everything right?

Oh, man.

Wheeler, you're an idiot, you know that?

Yeah, he did. He definitely knew that. Now. He only
hoped it wasn't too late for the lesson he'd just learned to
be put to good use. With one final glance around the office,
he pushed through the front door, locking it behind him.
And as he made his way to his car as quickly as he could,
he hoped like hell that luck—and love—was still with him.

And he wondered exactly how he was going to put both
to the best use.

Audrey Finnegan felt like the luckiest woman alive on
the planet. Everything in her life—every little, tiny, infinitesimal thing—was going perfectly. Exactly as she had
scripted it, ideal to the last detail. She was living precisely
as she wanted to live, finding happiness around every corner, indulging her every whim to its fullest extent. Every
dream she'd ever conjured had come true, every wish she'd
ever uttered had become reality, every desire she'd ever fed

was satisfied. Her mind, her spirit, her body, her very soul, were exactly as they should be. All was right in her world.

Until she woke up.

Audrey sighed heavily as her sleep-dazed eyes focused on the ceiling above her head. Then she rolled to her side and gazed dispassionately at the pale sunlight tumbling through the windows surrounding her bed. Every morning brought with it the same thing—consciousness. And with that consciousness came the memory of how Wheeler Rush had only wanted her in his life because she was his cursed good-luck charm.

Why should today be any different? she wondered. Did she really think her luck was going to change?

Every night when she fell asleep, she was assailed by dreams about him, dreams in which he came to her asking her to return to him, to never leave him, to stay with him forever and ever and ever. In those dreams the two of them made sweet, sensational love; they worked side by side at his office; they built an entire life together. And always, always, Wheeler wanted her close, because he couldn't live without her love.

Her love. Not her luck.

But that's all she had, night after night—dreams. Insubstantial, nocturnal, temporary. For weeks now, all she'd had to show for the months she'd spent with Wheeler were dreams. Well, dreams and the aching sense of loneliness and need that she was beginning to worry would never go away.

She told herself she was better off without him, that anything she and Wheeler might have shared together would have been doomed as long as he'd felt the way he had. It was just as well that their relationship had ended as it was budding, before it had a chance to blossom into something more. The pain would have only been worse had she spent more time with him, had she grown to love him more completely, had she come to trust him more fully.

Funny, though, how she really couldn't imagine the ache being any worse than it already was.

She reminded herself that her relationships with other men had ended far more messily, for far worse reasons than the fact that the man in question had only wanted her around because he thought she brought him good luck. Hey, at least Wheeler had viewed her in a positive light— even if it had been totally wrong and completely superficial. At least he'd thought of her as a good-luck charm instead of something like, oh, say...sushi.

Nevertheless, as she lay in her bed that Saturday morning, trying to rouse the wherewithal to rise and shine, Audrey had to admit that she was a lousy liar—even when it came to lying to herself. And as she lay there staring blindly at the windows, she could only feel the way she had felt for weeks. Empty. Sad. Lonely.

Yeah, looked like it was going to be another long day. Another long, hot day. Another long, hot, boring day full of nothing to do and nobody to do it with.

So why even bother getting out of bed? she thought. Hey, she could peruse the want ads for a job just as well from here as she could from anywhere. Of course, she'd have to get out of bed if she wanted to retrieve the Saturday paper from the hall. Feeling more put-upon than ever by that realization, Audrey forced herself into a sitting position and swung her legs over the side of the bed, not even bothering to look where she placed her feet.

She still hadn't quite gotten used to that. To not looking out where she was going. To not having to watch herself during her every waking moment. Anticipating an accident had always been second nature to her, because it had gone without saying that if there was an accident to be had, it would happen to a Finnegan. Upon waking every morning, she'd always been extra careful not to get tangled up in the sheets and fall out of bed or not to get a splinter from the hardwood floors or not to stub her toe on the way to the bathroom or not to spill hot coffee down the front of her dress.

But ever since making love with Wheeler, she hadn't had to worry about the kinds of things she used to worry about. Actually, it hadn't been *making* love with Wheeler that had been the turning point, she realized. It had been *falling* in love with him. For some reason, ever since she'd recognized her true feelings for him, she hadn't experienced any of the mishaps that had once been such a way of life for her. She hadn't tripped herself up or knocked herself down or suffered any of the bad luck that had always been a part of the Finnegan way of life.

Audrey still wasn't sure how or why that had happened. But somehow, by falling in love with Wheeler, by knowing that heartfelt, genuine, till-death-do-us-part kind of love for another human being, she had gained the kind of confidence and good karma necessary to overcome the misfortune that had dogged her all her life. Love had brought with it luck. And even if the love she felt for Wheeler hadn't been returned, the luck had stayed with her, as if it were some kind of a consolation prize, for what it was worth, and thanks so much for playing.

Audrey pushed a handful of dark curls out of her eyes as she made her way across the tiny apartment to her front door, pushing the button on the coffeemaker as she stumbled by it. She stretched languidly as a lusty yawn overtook her, then tugged ineffectually at the brief T-shirt she wore over her cotton panties in lieu of pajamas.

Since hers was the only apartment on the top floor of the house, she didn't worry about opening her front door long enough to grab the newspaper. Hey, after all, she was a lucky woman now, she reminded herself. No need to worry about getting caught with her pants down anymore. So to speak.

Unfortunately, Luck seemed to have other ideas for Audrey that morning. Because as she turned the knob to open her front door, stooping at the same time to scoop up the Saturday *Scene* as soon as the door was open, what she found on the floor wasn't her morning paper. It was a pair of shoes. Men's sneakers, to be precise. And there appeared to be a man standing in them.

The first thought that flitted through Audrey's head was that her luck had just been temporary and was taking a powder at the worst possible moment. Then she began to think that maybe, just maybe, the man who'd shown up on her doorstep was Wheeler Rush, and that maybe, just maybe, her luck was holding out better than she could ever have hoped.

She hoped.

Slowly, hungrily, she let her gaze rove up over the faded blue jeans molding strong calves and thighs. She speeded it up when she came to the man's pelvis, until she reached the flat planes of his torso encased in a tight-fitting T-shirt the color of a ripe avocado, then she let her gaze rove leisurely again. The taut fabric hugged the man's arms, delineating salient biceps and triceps that bunched and danced as he shifted her newspaper from one hand to the other. Tufts of dark hair sprung up from the shirt's crew neck, and above that was a strong throat and jaw freshly shaved.

The face above that, of course, was Wheeler's, but it looked different now from how it had the last time she'd seen him. When they had parted ways nearly a month before, his face had been lined with worry and tight with apprehension. Now, however, his eyes were lit with happiness. Happiness and something else, something she dared not try to identify. His lips—those sexy, luscious lips that had wreaked such havoc with her body—were curled into a smile, though that smile wasn't quite as cheerful as it could be.

He looked a bit tired, a bit weary, a bit concerned. But he didn't look like a man who was *completely* down on his luck.

"Hi," she said, still stooped before him, ignoring the fact that this probably wasn't a good pose for a woman in her position to be in. All things considered, Wheeler was really the one who should be poised for groveling.

"Hi," he replied, his expression growing a bit lighter.

She swallowed hard but said nothing more. Not because she couldn't think of anything to say—on the contrary there were a lot of things she'd wished she'd told him the last time she'd seen him, and they rose readily enough to mind now—but because she just wanted to look at him for a little while. It had been so long since she had been able to drink in the sight of him, so long since she'd had the chance to just gaze upon his face at her leisure.

And she promised herself then and there that if her luck held today, she would never take such simple pleasures for granted again.

He extended a hand to her, his fingers curled in invitation, and automatically she twined her fingers with his to let him pull her up. Effortlessly he tugged her to standing. But he didn't stop there, just kept pulling her forward, until her body was nestled easily against his. Before she could pull back—not that she necessarily wanted to pull back—he roped his arms around her waist and covered her mouth with his. And without a second's hesitation, Audrey melted into him.

His kiss was quite extraordinary, quite unlike anything she had ever experienced with a man before, Wheeler included. It was filled at once with certainty and solicitude, with passion and promise. It told Audrey that Wheeler had missed her—a lot—and that he had been none too sure what his reception would be when he arrived at her door.

Silly boy, she thought. He really could be an idiot sometimes.

As if he read her thoughts, he pulled back enough to gaze down into her face, and very quietly he said, "Audrey, I'm an idiot, did you know that?"

She smiled, a flicker of warmth curling in her stomach, licking at her insides with delicious heat. "Well, I might have had a couple of clues early on."

He chuckled softly. "Such as?"

"Well, for one thing, I could tell by your files that you needed to buy a clue."

He narrowed his eyes at her in confusion. "My files? But my files were perfectly well ordered. Hey, you could have eaten off my files."

She nodded. "That was the problem. I figured whoever worked as your secretary before me must have been a total file Nazi. And I figured anyone who was that anal about their files couldn't have been very good with people. And then I figured any boss who would hire a secretary who wasn't good with people could probably use a couple of pointers."

He smiled. "Or a better secretary."

"That, too."

His gaze locked with hers as he inhaled a deep breath and slowly released it. He lifted one hand to twine his fingers in her hair, and the other to brush the backs of his knuckles gently over one cheek. "Do you forgive me?" he asked.

Her heart hammered hard in her chest, but she was still afraid to hope for too much. "That depends," she said.

He continued to caress her face and hair, as if he couldn't quite bring himself to stop touching her. But his eyes never left hers as he asked, "On what?"

Audrey, too, lifted her hands to his face, cupping his rough jaws in her palms, strumming her thumbs along his strong cheekbones. "On what you're asking my forgiveness for."

He lowered his gaze as he opened his mouth to reply, and seemed to realize for the first time precisely how she was dressed. Or rather, precisely how she was *un*dressed.

"Uh, Audrey?" he asked.

"Yes?"

His gaze lingered at her waist, then dropped lower, to her bare legs. "You, uh…you don't seem to be wearing any clothes."

"Well, I did just sort of wake up a few minutes ago," she offered, by way of an explanation.

He nodded but didn't seem appeased by her response. "Oh. But, um…but you see…" Clearly with no small effort, he jerked his head up again, until his gaze settled on hers once more. "You, uh…you're not wearing any clothes," he repeated, as if that, above all else was of uppermost concern in his mind.

"Is that going to create a problem?" she asked.

"Well… It's just that… I mean… I had sort of intended for us to…you know…talk, and, uh…"

"So I can't talk to you in my underwear?"

"Well, of *course* you can talk to me in your underwear," he assured her. "I'm just not sure how much actual, uh…you know…talking…might get done, that's all."

"Well, there are those who would say that actions speak louder than words," she reminded him.

He nodded enthusiastically. "Yes. That's…that's certainly true. And believe me when I tell you that I do intend to offer some illustrations for what I'd like to say. But for now…"

She sighed with much disappointment. "Well, I guess if it's going to be that much of a distraction to you…"

He nodded vigorously. "Oh, believe me. It will definitely be a distraction."

"All right. I'll put on a robe."

But she made no move to comply with her decision, something Wheeler seemed to notice, because he drew his index finger along the line of her jaw, tracing her lower lip with his fingertips as he passed it. "I suppose I should thank you for that, but for some reason, I feel in no way grateful."

She smiled again and tried to ignore the irregular fluttering of her heartbeat, then pushed herself up on tiptoe to brush her mouth lightly over his. Just when he started to kiss her back, however, she pulled herself away. No sense starting something they might not be able to finish. In spite of his gestures of affection, she hadn't heard what he'd come to tell her. And although she'd made a halfhearted effort to put that discussion off, she knew they really did need to talk.

"Come on in," she said.

She turned and left him to enter and close the door behind himself, then donned the short, flowered kimono that lay in the chair near her bed. The coffee had finished brewing by then, so she offered him a cup...and wasn't much surprised when he declined. Filling one for herself, she made her way to the living room, to where Wheeler sat on the sofa, gazing at her. He leaned forward, hooking his hands together between his knees, and never took his eyes off of her for a second. She seated herself in a chair opposite him, placing her coffee on the end table beside her, and eyed him back in silent expectation.

"I've missed you, Audrey," he said without preamble.

She parted her lips in surprise, but no words emerged to describe her reaction. Which wasn't surprising, considering the fact that she wasn't sure *how* to describe the turmoil of emotions rising and swirling inside her.

As if he couldn't sit still, Wheeler rose then, and paced to the opposite side of the room. Then he spun around and made his way back to the couch. But he didn't sit down. Instead he faced Audrey as if she were his executioner, dropping his hands to his sides.

"It took me a while to figure things out," he began again, "but once I did, I realized you were right. About a lot of things. Mainly you were right about the fact that I was an idiot. Because I was."

"You were?"

He nodded. "But I'm not anymore. I finally understand what you were trying to tell me that last day, just before you walked out on me."

Audrey felt herself blush. "I didn't walk out on you, Wheeler," she said. "I quit my job."

He eyed her levelly. "Please tell me you haven't found a new one yet."

She decided she didn't like the way that sounded, and wondered exactly where he was headed with his remark. "Why?" she asked warily.

"Because I want to hire you back."

Just like that, all of her fragile hopes shattered, and all of her tentative dreams dissolved. This was why he'd come over? she thought. To offer her a job again? She expelled a soft, incredulous sound. He really was an idiot.

"Wheeler—"

"It's not what you think," he interrupted her. He held up one hand, palm out. "Just hear me out, okay?"

She nodded miserably. "Yeah, okay. Whatever."

He began to pace again, but there was less restlessness in the action now. He seemed more thoughtful, more careful, more intent. "As I said, you were right about a lot of things. But there was one thing you were definitely wrong about. You *were* responsible for the success and downfall of my business. It was you, Audrey, who made the difference. You. When I had you in my employ, the business grew beautifully. Without you, it hasn't grown at all."

She closed her eyes and fought the tears that threatened. Not again. Not that stupid good-luck charm stuff again. How could he do this to her?

"But now I realize that wasn't because you brought me good luck," he said.

She snapped her eyes open, but didn't dare let herself hope. "What?"

"I said you weren't my good-luck charm," he reiterated. "I realize that now. It wasn't because you were lucky that the business did well. It was because you're good with people."

She was still confused. "Come again?" she said.

He smiled, crossed the room one final time and stooped in front of her in that position of groveling she had supposed he should be in before. But instead of groveling, he took her hands in his and smiled.

"You're good with people," he said again. "My clients loved you. They responded to you. I finally understand that the reason I didn't lose clients while you were onboard, why I signed so many *new* clients while you were onboard, *wasn't* so much because of my knowledge or my skill or my talent—or my luck, for that matter. It was because you were able to talk people into giving me a chance. You made them feel better about the business, about me." He shrugged immodestly. "Sure, my knowledge and skill and talent was important, but it was that human factor that you provided that made all the difference."

"Oh, come on," she objected lightly. "I didn't do anything anybody else couldn't do."

His gaze was earnest as he assured her, "Oh, yes, you did. Rosalie, my former secretary, the one you called a file Nazi? You're right—she wasn't much of a people person. In fact, I think she drove away more business that I realized because she was so abrasive and unconcerned about anything but the files and the state of office affairs. She was a whiz keeping things in order, but no good at dealing with clients. You, however, are a warm and wonderful human being to whom others simply respond well. And because of that, people wanted to do business with Rush Commercial Designs.

"It wasn't the fact that you were a good-luck charm that led to things going so well for me, for the business," he added, smiling. "It was the fact that you're a nice person, and people like you."

"But—"

"And, considering your abundant skills in that department," he hurried on, "I'd like to hire you back. In a capacity other than secretary."

Once again, the hopes and dreams that Audrey had begun to build slowly began to crumble. It all came down to business with him, she thought. That was why he'd come. Maybe he didn't view her as a good-luck charm anymore, but he didn't view her as a love interest, either. He wanted her back, sure. Because, just like before, she'd be an asset to the company.

She tugged her hands free of his as she rose to stand. "Wheeler, I don't think—"

"Come back to me, Audrey," he said. But he didn't rise with her. He had settled on one knee before her, and on one knee before her was where he stayed.

"Thanks, but—"

"As my partner," he interjected.

"I don't think—"

"As my wife."

"I just don't—"

She snapped her head down to look at him so fast she almost got reverse whiplash. "Come again?"

He smiled. "Be my partner," he repeated.

"No, not that part," she told him. "The other part."

His smile grew broader. "Be my wife."

She gaped at him.

"Audrey Finnegan," he said, his eyes dancing with a merry, mischievous light, "I'm doing this the best way I know how." He reached up and took one of her hands in his, then, smiling, he asked, "Will you marry me?"

"Marry you?" she gasped. "Are you serious? You want to marry me? *Me*?"

"I'm very serious," he assured her. "Of course I want to marry you."

"Why?"

He arrowed his eyebrows downward, clearly feigning

deep concentration. "Let's see now... I knew the answer to that a minute ago... What was it...? Oh, yeah. I remember now." His brow cleared, and he gazed up at her again with warm, wistful, wonderful eyes. "Because I love you."

"But—"

"And I can't live my life without you."

"But—"

"And if I had you by my side, I'd be the luckiest man alive."

Her entire body went rigid. She couldn't believe her ears. Would he never stop harping on that? "Oh, Wheeler, not that. Not again. Please."

"Hey, I'm sorry, but any man who has the love of Audrey Finnegan is, without question, the most fortunate man in the world. You're just going to have to accept that, sweetheart, and learn to live with it. Because it's true."

Once again her hopes and dreams flickered to life. "But I'm jinxed," she said, knowing that wasn't really true. Not anymore. She just wanted to make extra sure. "I'm hexed. Star-crossed. Fortune's fool and all that."

"I don't care about the long history of Finnegan bad luck," he said. "You and I, Audrey, we'll make our own luck. And it will all be good."

"How do you figure?"

"Because with the love we have for each other—and I'm betting you do still love me, because you have that look in your eyes—there can only be good fortune ahead. It's that simple."

She smiled. "You think so?"

He nodded, clearly resolved to this line of thinking. "I know so. Luck, I've learned—the hard way, I might add—doesn't come from a magic charm. It comes in the form of a personal outlook. Positive thinking. Optimism. That kind of thing. I'd lost that optimistic outlook on life, and that was why my business started to suffer. Then, when you came into my life, everything changed.

"Not because you were lucky for me," he added quickly, when she opened her mouth to object, "but because you loved me. Because I loved you. Whether I realized it or not, I did fall in love with you pretty fast. And when I did, suddenly, anything seemed possible. Without you, I felt helpless, hopeless. And things naturally declined.

"It was you all along, Audrey," he concluded his analysis. "Because all along, I loved you. I was just too stupid to realize it until it was almost too late."

She only gazed at him in confusion and said nothing, not sure how to respond.

And at her silence Wheeler's smile fell. "It's not too late, is it?" he asked. "You do still love me? Don't you?"

To that, Audrey definitely knew how to respond. And as she'd said before, actions spoke louder than words. So she reached for the belt of her robe and deftly untied it, then shrugged the garment from her shoulders.

Okay, Wheeler thought as the delicate fabric pooled around Audrey's ankles, brushing his face as it went, he was pretty sure that qualified as a positive response. Just to be certain, however, and not wanting to waste what he'd realized was a really good position to be in, he reached for her hips and pulled her forward, pressing his mouth to the soft line of silky skin revealed between her panties and T-shirt.

"Tell me you love me," he murmured against her heated flesh.

"I love you," she said, the words coming out thready and warm. She twined her fingers in his hair. "I love you so much."

He still wasn't convinced his luck was going to hold, so he traced the delicate line of her navel with the tip of his tongue and added, "Say you'll marry me."

He felt her fingers tighten in his hair. "I'll marry you," she said sweetly.

It was all the assurance he needed. Splaying his hands

open over the small of her back, Wheeler nudged her body forward and dragged open-mouthed kisses along the exposed portion of her torso. Very quickly, however, he realized that wasn't going to be nearly enough to satisfy the roar of desire that had soared up inside him the moment he'd lain eyes on her at her front door. So he scooped his hands inside her panties, palming the firm globes of her bottom before pushing the soft fabric down over her thighs.

Her dusky scent assaulted him as she stepped out of her panties, and he dropped his kisses lower, to the damp, downy curls between her legs. He heard her gasp something incoherent, some halfhearted protest that he knew she didn't mean, because even as she uttered it, she took a step to the side to spread her legs wider for him. He accepted the invitation readily, dipped his head lower still, and laved the heated heart of her.

"Oh," she moaned above him. "Oh, Wheeler."

He gripped her taut buttocks more firmly, pushing her toward his marauding mouth, tasting her as deeply as he could. For long moments, he feasted upon her, trying to satisfy a ravenous hunger he hadn't fed for weeks. Only when Audrey's legs buckled beneath her did he cease his assault, catching her capably in his hands.

He scooped her into his arms as he stood, and carried her to her bed, its sheets still rumpled from what had clearly been a restless night's sleep. He smiled. Good. He was glad to know he wasn't the only one who'd been suffering tumultuous dreams these past few weeks.

Without comment, he laid her down on the bed, pushing her shirt up over her breasts, too anxious, too hungry, to worry about removing the garment. He went to work on the buttons of his fly as he bent over her and drew the rosy peak of one breast into his mouth, sucking as much of her ripe flesh as he could, laving her nipple with his tongue. He felt her hands join his, pushing at his blue jeans, tugging them and his briefs down over his thighs.

And then, unable to tolerate the separation of their bodies any longer, he spread her legs and propelled himself deep inside her, thrusting as hard, as far, as fast as he could. She gasped at his fleet, furious possession, then immediately matched his rhythm. Cupping both of her hands behind his nape, she pulled his head down to hers, covering his mouth, thrusting her tongue inside to mimic the actions of his body within hers. She possessed him as completely as he had taken her. He belonged to her. And she to him.

He pushed and pushed until both of them reached their limit. And then, in a burst of white-hot intensity, he felt the ripples of satisfaction just out of reach. Faster and faster he drove himself inside her, crying out as she matched his actions with her own body, bucking hard against him. As one, they reached that pinnacle of fulfillment, and they clung to each other to keep from falling apart. Then, as quickly as the heat had arisen, it abated, and they lay together, spent and exhausted.

"Never leave me," Audrey whispered against the damp skin of his neck.

"I never will. Stay with me always."

"You know I will. I love you."

"I love you."

And that, Wheeler knew, was all that he would ever need in his life.

Epilogue

As always, things were hopping in the expanded Main Street offices of Rush-Finnegan Designs, Inc. But that wasn't exactly surprising. The newly reorganized company was the talk of the town, after all, and its partners' faces had been splashed on the front page of every business publication in three states. And their reputation was growing every day, because Rush-Finnegan Designs was known not just for their cutting-edge ideas, but for their ability to keep all of their clients extremely happy. They were by far the savviest—and the luckiest—designers around.

Audrey sighed with contentment as she watched the furniture movers carry her new desk into her new office—the one next to Wheeler's that was connected by an adjoining door. Her black jeans and snug, cropped black sweater were in no way comparable to her usual working attire, but it was Saturday, and the office was closed. Still, she wanted to make sure everything was in order for their official grand reopening Monday morning.

"To the left a little," she told the movers, waving her hand negligently in that direction. Then she halted the gesture abruptly. "No, wait…to the right. A little more…a little more… There. Perfect. Right in front of the window. That's it."

The burly men set the desk down with a gentleness completely at odds with their size and appearance. In spite of the chilly November breeze whiffling through the open window behind him, the larger of the two mopped the perspiration from his brow with a faded blue bandanna. "There you go, Ms. Finnegan-Rush," he said. "You're all set for business."

No matter how often anyone spoke words to that effect, Audrey thought, she would never grow tired of hearing them. "Thanks, Bruno," she said with a smile. "I appreciate it. And if you ever need commercial design work done, you know where to come."

He smiled back as he returned the bandanna to his trouser pocket. "Oh, you betcha." As he and his companion exited, he called back over his shoulder, "Good luck with the new digs."

Audrey murmured her thanks in response, appreciating his good wishes. However, she knew they were completely unnecessary. She already had all the luck she would ever need. Because she had Wheeler's love, and that was all that mattered.

"Everything set to go?"

As if conjured by her thoughts, Wheeler stuck his head through the door that joined her office to his, and Audrey bit back a sigh at the sight of him. In his workday uniform of suit and tie, her husband was, hands-down, the best-looking hunka man going. But dressed as he was now, in faded, form-fitting Levi's and a dusky gray sweatshirt whose sleeves were pushed up to his elbows, he was... He was...

Whoa. That was what he was.

Somehow she willed her wildly thumping heart not to jump right out of her chest. "Just call me Madame Vice President," she said in response to his question.

He smiled as he strode through the door and into her new office. "I'd rather call you my wife," he said easily.

She wiggled her eyebrows playfully, then crossed the office to meet him halfway. Pushing herself up on tiptoe when she reached him, she said, "I'd rather you call me your..." Her voice trailed off into a whisper, but she knew Wheeler heard what she said, because his face flushed with heat and his entire body went taut.

"Ah, yeah. Well. I could call you that," he said agreeably, snaking his arm around her waist to pull her close. He cupped a hand over her cheek, drove his fingers into her hair and brushed his lips along the sleek line of her jaw. "Then again," he murmured softly, "I think actions speak louder than words, don't you?"

"Oh," she said on a sigh as his other hand crept up over her rib cage to settle under the lower curve of her breast. "Oh, yeah. Definitely." She swallowed with some difficulty, then lifted a hand to his hair, feathering her fingers through the dark, silky tresses. "But you know what they say about those office romances," she added, feigning concern.

He nuzzled her neck, and her heart hammered double time. "No, what?"

She chuckled low. "They're everything they're cracked up to be."

"And then some," he agreed, covering her breast completely, palming it possessively as he nibbled the tender flesh revealed by the scooped neck of her sweater. "Audrey," he said softly, skimming his mouth lightly up and down along the column of her throat.

"Hmm...?" she asked, suddenly feeling distracted for some reason.

He nibbled her skin some more before observing, "You know, that's an awfully big desk you bought for your office."

She smiled. "Mmm-hmm. I know."

He nipped her earlobe, then dipped his head lower, to taste the creamy flesh of her nape. "Really," he said softly, "when you get right down to it, you could do all kinds of things with a desk that claimed that much square footage."

A sizzle of electricity ignited in all the places where he touched her, shimmying through her entire body as he continued with his exploration. "Mmm-hmm," she agreed. "You could. You're right."

"Design new ideas," he went on heedlessly, his fingers creeping down now, toward the hem of her sweater. When he arrived at his destination, he deftly ducked his hand inside.

"Mmm-hmm," she said again.

"Place orders for all kinds of things we'll be needing as the business grows."

"Mmm-hmm..."

"Work on all those public relations projects you've come up with to keep our clients happy."

"Mmm-hmm..."

"Make savage love to your husband."

She laughed, a sexy, sensuous sound, and reached for the hem of his sweatshirt, shoving both of her hands inside to investigate all the bumps and ridges of muscle beneath. "Why do you think I went with that particular model?" she asked smoothly.

He grinned. "Maybe we ought to give it a test run before you get it all cluttered up with computers and blotters and calendars and stuff like that."

"Sounds great," she said agreeably, tugging his shirt up over his head and tossing it to the floor. Then, without hesitation, she went after the buttons on his jeans. "Just one question."

He, too, wrestled her sweater up over her head and cast it aside. Then he covered both breasts, clad in a wisp of black lace, with sure fingers. "Yes?" he said as he pushed his hands together and upward, lowering his head to the lush flesh that spilled out of her bra with the gesture.

"Oh," she whispered at the feel of his damp mouth on her breasts. "Who...who gets to drive?" she managed to ask.

He laughed low, the vibration generating an even greater heat and demand inside her. "Well, Madame Vice President," he said, "you're the one who's in charge of keeping the clients happy. You might as well get used to performing the same service for your business partner. Which, as we both know, would be me."

"I can keep you happy," she said breathlessly. And there wasn't an ounce of uncertainty in the statement. She finished with his buttons, then tucked her fingers inside his jeans to cup him with *much* affection.

"Oh," he said as she brushed her fingers along the solid, ample length of him. "That you can. No complaints there."

"And I know you're going to make me happy, too, aren't you?"

He nodded. "Very, very happy."

She smiled. "Then you can drive. The first time."

"I thought you'd never ask."

As Wheeler began a slow, sensuous dance back toward her desk, Audrey realized she didn't have any complaints, either. Hey, who could complain about getting everything you'd ever wanted or wished for in your entire life? As far as she was concerned, Audrey Finnegan-Rush was the most fortunate woman alive.

And there in her new office, with the autumn sun tumbling through the window in a bright, shining promise of all the good things that lay ahead of them, Audrey and Wheeler did everything within their power to ensure that they always got lucky.

*   *   *   *   *

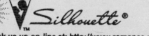

If you enjoyed what you just read,
then we've got an offer you can't resist!

Take 2 bestselling
love stories FREE!
Plus get a FREE surprise gift!

Clip this page and mail it to Silhouette Reader Service™

IN U.S.A.	IN CANADA
3010 Walden Ave.	P.O. Box 609
P.O. Box 1867	Fort Erie, Ontario
Buffalo, N.Y. 14240-1867	L2A 5X3

YES! Please send me 2 free Silhouette Desire® novels and my free surprise gift. Then send me 6 brand-new novels every month, which I will receive months before they're available in stores. In the U.S.A., bill me at the bargain price of $3.12 plus 25¢ delivery per book and applicable sales tax, if any*. In Canada, bill me at the bargain price of $3.49 plus 25¢ delivery per book and applicable taxes**. That's the complete price and a savings of over 10% off the cover prices—what a great deal! I understand that accepting the 2 free books and gift places me under no obligation ever to buy any books. I can always return a shipment and cancel at any time. Even if I never buy another book from Silhouette, the 2 free books and gift are mine to keep forever. So why not take us up on our invitation. You'll be glad you did!

225 SEN CNFA
326 SEN CNFC

Name	(PLEASE PRINT)	
Address		Apt.#
City	State/Prov.	Zip/Postal Code

* Terms and prices subject to change without notice. Sales tax applicable in N.Y.
** Canadian residents will be charged applicable provincial taxes and GST.
 All orders subject to approval. Offer limited to one per household.
® are registered trademarks of Harlequin Enterprises Limited.

DES99   ©1998 Harlequin Enterprises Limited

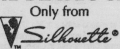